The Soul Whisperer's Decision

The **Soul** Whisperer's Decision

By

Gwen M. Plano

Fresh Ink Group
Guntersville

The Soul Whisperer's Decision

Fresh Ink Group
An Imprint of:
The Fresh Ink Group, LLC
1021 Blount Avenue #931
Guntersville, AL 35976
Email: info@FreshInkGroup.com
FreshInkGroup.com

Edition 1.0 2024

Cover design by Stephen Geez / FIG
Book design by Amit Dey / FIG
Associate publisher Beem Weeks / FIG

Cataloging-in-Publication Recommendations:
FIC009050 FICTION / Fantasy / Paranormal
FIC026000 FICTION / Religious
FIC031070 FICTION / Thrillers / Supernatural

Library of Congress Control Number: 2023921842

ISBN-13: 978-1-958922-62-0 Papercover
ISBN-13: 978-1-958922-63-7 Hardcover
ISBN-13: 978-1-958922-64-4 Ebooks

ACKNOWLEDGEMENTS

THE SOUL WHISPERER'S DECISION is a piece of fiction written out of the author's imagination. Arizona and Spain are real locations with real people, but the events described, characters developed, and places visited are purely fictional with no intent to depict reality.

The real folks are those who worked diligently behind the scenes to bring *THE SOUL WHISPERER'S DECISION* to readers. My deepest *thank you* extends to Justina M. Aguirre for her guidance with the medical scenes. As a retired nurse and academic dean, she provided the expertise I do not have. I also thank my editor for her tireless efforts on my behalf, and I am deeply grateful to the dedicated team at Fresh Ink Group. Finally, a very special *thank you* goes to my husband for his loving and patient encouragement. Thank you all.

QUOTE

Love is our true destiny.
We do not find the meaning of life by
ourselves alone - we find it with another.

Thomas Merton

TABLE OF CONTENTS

CHAPTER 1

THE ACCIDENT

A red playground ball bounces in front of Sarah while she wanders home after an eight-hour shift at County Central Hospital. She chuckles and turns to look for the children who sent the ball her way. Three boys scramble toward her, laughing as they run. Sarah joins in the revelry, throws the ball back to the kids, and lets go of the tensions of a busy Saturday in the Emergency Room.

After a deep breath, Sarah unties her shoulder-length auburn hair and runs her hands through the curls. Her thoughts shift to grocery shopping—her usual Saturday chore. Detergent, trash bags, baby formula . . . the list is long. She wonders about dinner and decides to surprise Jack, her husband of five years, with his favorite meal—lasagna and fresh vegetables. Absorbed in her plans, she jumps when a neighbor shouts, "*Hello.*"

Sarah twists around. "Hey, Jane, what are you up to?"

"Same ol', same ol'. Just puttering around in the garden. These weeds keep me busy. How about you? Usually, you don't work weekends. Is everything okay at the hospital?"

"Yeah, everything's fine. You're right, normally I don't work weekends. A fellow nurse had some family obligations to attend to, so I volunteered. But now it's playtime with the kids and Jack. Speaking of them, I better get going. I'll see you later. Don't work too hard. It must be in the high eighties out here."

Sarah continues on her way and glances across the street at her small ranch home. Weeds wave at her in mockery from the front yard. Between work and the kids, Jack and she rarely have time for maintenance and gardening. *Someday, maybe.* She smiles at three-year-old Bobby's tricycle under the cypress tree, and the baby's stroller, which rests next to the front steps. *Weeds or not, there's no place like home. It's a sanctuary like none other.*

Sarah walks up the two steps to the front door, and little Bobby rushes out.

"Mommy, Mommy!"

"Hey, partner." She rubs his carroty mane. "Have you been a good boy for your daddy?"

"Yes, Mommy, I was verrry good."

"Well, I guess you deserve a surprise from the grocery store."

"Can I go? Can I go?" He jumps up and down.

"Let's ask Daddy first, and if he's okay with it, then you can go."

When Sarah steps inside the house, Jack wraps one arm around her and holds eight-month-old Marci in his other. "Rough day?"

"Not at all. The usual ups and downs. How did you do with the kids?"

Teasingly, Jack rolls his eyes. "Well, let's see. Bobby taught me his ABCs song. And I can now count to ten. And I know the difference between a circle and a triangle. I'd say I'm a fast learner. And Marci? Well, I must have changed her diapers a dozen times. That kid drinks too much."

Sarah laughs, brushes her husband's tousled chestnut hair away from his face, and strokes the battle scar that runs down his cheek. "It can't be as bad as Afghanistan. Though, I admit, the two of them make quite the team. I'll take the kids with me to the store. You deserve a break."

Jack sets the baby on the floor and pulls Sarah close. "I've waited all day for this hug. By the way, you're right about the *team*. Taking care of both kids makes my eight-to-five job feel like a vacation."

Sarah reaches up for a kiss. "Give me an hour, and I'll have a great meal on the table—with your favorite dessert. If you can get the kids fastened into their seat belts, I'll change quickly and get on my way."

"I'm on it!" Jack picks up Marci and calls out to Bobby to follow him.

Sarah dashes into the bedroom, where she takes off her nursing scrubs, tosses them toward the hamper where only her uniforms go, and grabs a T-shirt and a pair of jeans. After slipping on her sandals, she's ready.

She walks outside just as Jack closes the back doors of their maroon sedan. "They're both fastened into their car seats, and I've got them singing the alphabet song—again." He raises his eyebrows and brings Sarah close for a final hug.

"I'll be back in a couple. Maybe we can relax tonight with a glass of wine." She teases him with a peck on the cheek.

Sarah backs out of the driveway and heads down their tree-lined street, mentally rehearsing her list of needed household items. It's only a short jaunt to the grocery store, but the shift from hospital obligations to household tasks refreshes her spirit. Along the way, Sarah recognizes a few neighbors and waves, and they return the gesture. Bobby waves from the back seat and loudly sings his alphabet song. Amused, Sarah laughs lightheartedly and joins him. When Marci chimes in with her baby words, Sarah contemplates how blessed she is. *A perfect day*, she thinks. She pulls up to the red light and offers a quick prayer of thanksgiving.

Then the unthinkable happens.

The traffic light turns green, and Sarah releases her brakes and eases into the cross street. At that moment, a furniture delivery truck barrels through its red light and hits them squarely on the side. The impact throws the vehicle in the air and against a stone retaining wall.

··•✦•✦•••··

Jack and the neighbors hear the crash of metal against metal, of glass shattering and horns sounding, and run to the intersection. The young father's expression turns to horror when he reaches the scene. He tries to open the door to the crumpled, overturned car to free his wife and their children, all the while crying out for help.

Men dash to his aid and rock the car in an attempt to get it upright. The strobes of police lights and howls of sirens move the crowd of onlookers to the side of the street. Firefighters wrench Jack away from the vehicle and tell the bystanders to stand back so they can work. With the Jaws of Life, the firemen cut through the damaged door to reach the trapped family.

One by one, the paramedics retrieve the toddler and the infant and commence cardiopulmonary resuscitation. Another two firemen work to free Sarah. When they finally pull her from the rubble, she's unresponsive, pulseless, and bleeding profusely from an obvious head injury. They administer CPR immediately. Unable to get a heartbeat, they stop.

Jack begs them to continue, "She's strong, she can make it. Please, don't stop. Please."

For his sake, they continue, and to everyone's surprise, a heartbeat registers. The medical team loads Sarah into the ambulance and speeds away. At the blare of the sirens, Jack presses his hands against his ears and wails in denial. Over and over again, he thinks, *This can't be real. This can't be real.*

Then he refocuses on the babies, spins around, and freezes. His precious little ones are covered with a blanket.

"No, no, no!" He falls to his knees and cries out in despair. A neighbor kneels beside him and tries to console him, but Jack pays no heed. He reaches for Bobby, rocks the lifeless child, then lays him back down and picks up Marci. Back and forth he sways, pleading for help. A female responder crouches beside him and talks with him in soothing tones. Eventually, he lets go of the baby and covers his face with his hands.

Minutes later, the coroner arrives. Solemnly, he plods over to the police officers, who point to the grieving father on his knees beside the two covered tiny bodies. The man nods his understanding and walks to Jack's side. He places his arm around the tearful man's shoulder and says, "I can't imagine the pain you must feel. Your two beautiful children are no longer with us." The coroner clenches his jaw and rubs Jack's back. "This is every parent's worst fear. My heart breaks for you."

Jack's head falls with the burden of his devastation.

"My name's Simon Westerly. I'm the coroner. I need to take your beloved angels with me. When we have any fatality caused by a car accident, the law requires us to investigate."

Jack kneads the sides of his face and sobs. His shoulders convulse with the weight of unprocessed sorrow.

"I will take good care of your children and prepare them for the mortuary. Please, take this card and call me if you have any questions. Could I have your cell number?"

Jack mutters a reply.

"Could you repeat that please?"

The mourning father lifts his head slightly and repeats his number.

This time, Simon understands. "One more thing—you'll need a personal injury lawyer to help you with what lies ahead. Ask your friends for a referral or give me a call, and I'll help you locate one."

Jack nods without raising his eyes and acknowledges the stranger's advice with a simple, "Thank you."

CHAPTER 2

THE SURGERY

The ambulance screeches to a stop at the hospital emergency entrance with alarms blasting. The first responders had called ahead to alert the hospital of the gravity of the victim's condition, and a doctor and several nurses stand ready to rush the patient to surgery. Grabbing the gurney, the medical team pushes it through the fluorescent-lit hallway and into the elevator to the fifth floor. The blood-covered body is unrecognizable.

As they ascend, a neurosurgeon prepares his unit for what lies ahead—possible damage to both the brain and spine. He explains the risks and the urgency of time.

"What do we know about the patient?"

A nurse reads from the directive, "Two-vehicle incident. Female, twenty-six-years-old, mother of two. Her name is . . ." The nurse stops and stares at the surgeon. "Dr. Roberts, this is Sarah Jameson."

The surgeon's mouth falls open. "I was just with her an hour ago."

"The collision happened only a block from her home, according to the paramedic."

The doctor gasps his words, "That's, that's unbelievable."

When the elevator stops, they rush the gurney through the surgery doors. Dr. Roberts calls out, "Be ready in five. She's between life and death. We've got to move quickly. This is no ordinary surgery. The patient is our beloved friend."

A tech adjusts the surgical light and positions the mobile C-arm X-ray at an angle next to the operating table, which will assist the surgeon with the delicate procedures. The anesthesiologist checks and rechecks his monitors and makes sure the fluid bags and blood products hang ready.

The heart monitor sounds. "She's flatlined. She's flatlined," the nurse anesthetist calls out. Staff move swiftly and attach a defibrillator. On the first shock, no response. Second shock, no response.

"We've lost her, Doctor. We've lost her."

Roberts furrows his brow and sets his jaw. "Another shock." "Again." No response. "Again." No response.

The attending nurses wait for Dr. Roberts to give the signal. The anesthesiologist moves next to him and says in a low voice, "She's gone."

Roberts winces and white-knuckles his fists. Reluctantly, he calls the time: 6:15 p.m. While he paces back and forth, he yanks off his gloves and tosses them into a bin forcefully. He starts to pull off his mask and surgical cap, but then a nurse screams.

"She's alive. I saw the sheet move."

Roberts darts to Sarah's side. "The monitor. Turn it on!" Intently, he focuses on the screen. "There's a pulse." He swivels to his team. "Let's do this. We must act immediately."

After re-donning his protective gear, the surgeon waits for the signal from his teammates. When he sees they're ready, he begins.

··✦·✦·✦·✦·✦··

Four hours later, Dr. Roberts straightens. "Good work, all. The next few hours are critical, but we've given her a fighting chance." He closes his eyes momentarily and wipes the beads of sweat from his forehead. Glancing over to the anesthesiologist, he nods and says, "Thank you."

With those few words, Dr. Roberts leaves to speak with Jack. He finds him in the surgical waiting room, slumped with his head cupped in his hands. He clears his throat and says, "Jack, I have some hopeful news."

The young man sits up and, with red swollen eyes, he says, "Yes?"

"It's still tenuous, but I'm hopeful. With a traumatic brain injury, healing can be slow. I dislodged a small fragment of bone and believe there will be no permanent damage. Her lower spine, however, suffered severe trauma. Fortunately, the cord was not severed. This gives me hope, and I believe, in time, she'll walk again."

"What do you mean by *in time?*"

"She's in an unconscious state, so I can't measure the degree of damage. But all things considered, I believe she'll move freely in a couple of months with the help of physical therapy."

"When can I visit her?"

"Not tonight, maybe tomorrow. She needs to remain in the Neuro-Intensive Care unit, and because of her fragile state, we can't risk introducing contagion. Go home and rest. You've been through a lot today, and you need to recover your strength. Tomorrow we may know more."

CHAPTER 3

THE EMPTY HOME

A passing car backfires as Jack exits the hospital. Quickly, he ducks behind the entrance post and readies for combat. In his mind, he's in an Afghan village, leading a platoon assigned to check Taliban hiding places in a neighborhood.

He kicks open the door to a suspect home and discovers the roof ripped apart from the shelling. With assault weapons shouldered, he and his team charge in. They find no insurgents, but two children lie lifeless next to their mother. Jack yells to the combat medic for help, but he's too late.

Jack startles from his inner post-war experience when an ambulance drives past. Hyperventilating, he questions, *What's happening to me?* He grabs his chest and tells himself to get a grip. Stooped with eyes focused on the ground, he crosses the street, oblivious of cars. A driver honks his horn and yells, "Hey, crazy man, get out of the way!" Jack staggers to the sidewalk, caught between worlds, with only misery pumping through his broken heart.

Barely visible on this moonless night, the house that once was a home looms in front of Jack. He stiffens and squares his shoulders. Ascending the steps, he rests his forehead on the weathered door. *They're all gone. I'm alone. The house has become my sepulcher.* He takes a few deep inhalations and confronts the desolate abode. A message taped against the wooden door frame gives him pause. Jack yanks it off, shoves it into his pocket, and opens the door.

A chilly silence greets him. He flips on the lights and the scattered remains of a once-happy family immobilize him. Toys lay, randomly, on the floor. Baby bottles sit in the sink. A half-full cup of coffee rests on the table. All as he and his wife left them five hours earlier.

Grim images parade through his pounding heart. His lifeless babies and Sarah covered in blood. All the horror flashes repeatedly in his mind. He rehashes what went wrong. *If only I'd kept the kids at home with me. If only I'd shopped for groceries earlier today. If only . . . if only I died with them.* He smashes his fist against the wall. *Why? Why am I the one left behind?* He sucks in a breath and wishes he had none.

Jack's hand trembles when he closes the front door behind him. Again, he's on the battlefield. He hears the air raid and darts into the darkness, only to find the horrifying roar of *emptiness*. Gasping with each inhalation, he finds himself back at the accident. His little ones lie motionless before him, his wife teeters between life and oblivion. He is alone—with only fear for company.

He pulls the wrinkled message from his pocket. It's from the police department, and it tells him to call the listed number. With his jaw clamped tight, Jack punches in the digits. After a few questions, he learns that a drunken driver hit his family. Charged with first-degree vehicular manslaughter, the man remains behind bars. Jack listens to the words but they don't sink in. Detail after detail travels past him until, through his emotional daze, he hears, "There was nothing your wife could have done to protect herself and the kids. Her fate would have been ours if we were driving the car. The truck hit her without any warning. She never saw it."

The grief-stricken father says, "And she'll never hold her babies again."

Jack collapses on the threadbare couch and grips his head as he yells into the somber abyss, *This is not real. It can't be.* In his mind's eye, the Afghani children stand before him—again—but this time, his precious little ones stand next to them. *It shouldn't have happened. Innocents killed. For what? A Taliban insurgent's vengeance? A drunk driver's pint of whiskey? The children are victims of evil.* Jack pulls in a breath, fingers his phone, and calls his only sibling.

"Sis . . ."

"Jack, what's wrong? What's happened?"

"The babies . . ." he chokes out.

"What about them?" She waits and then says forcefully, "Jack, speak to me!"

"They're dead, Chrissy."

"What? Are you serious? I was with them yesterday. How? When?"

"Accident. Five hours ago. Sarah's unconscious. In intensive care. Traumatic brain injury. A truck hit the car. Drunken driver arrested."

"Jack, I'll be at the house in ten minutes."

"No. Please, don't. I've . . . I've got to be alone."

"Tomorrow morning then."

"I'll leave the back door unlocked, in case I'm at the hospital when you arrive."

Jack ends the call and staggers to the bedroom. His eyes dart across the forsaken space. Sarah's blue scrubs lay lifeless on the hamper's edge, her nursing shoes tossed to the side. The top drawer of her dresser hangs ajar, just as she left it. And, on the nightstand, Sarah's diary. It rests open, facing down. He walks over to the journal and reads the last entry. *When I put Marci to bed tonight, she whispered, "I love you, Mommy," then drifted to sleep. My tears gathered at the purity of her words. A child doesn't know the power of love. They simply live it.*

The grieving husband shouts out his pain to no one and pants fast breaths. "I can't sleep in here tonight. It feels like it's closing in on me." Bent over, he finds a blanket and sprints out of the suffocating room.

Unfortunately, as soon as he switches on the TV, Jack hears Sarah's name. He sits up to watch the news feed and sees a tow truck lift his mangled sedan onto the flatbed. He scans the gathered crowds. Some people point, others cry, but all look horrified. He recognizes Jane, their neighbor from across the street. And he glimpses Fred, his backyard buddy, wiping his eyes.

The reporter interrupts and shares an earlier clip. In this video, three police officers tackle and cuff a burly man in overalls. Jack studies the criminal who killed his babies and hollers aloud at the monster. In a rage, he throws a couch pillow at the television and yells, "WHY? WHY?" He listens to the reporter's comments for a few more minutes, then—unable to take any more—he turns off the TV, drops his head into his hands, and sobs. Finally, he confesses, "I wish I was the one pronounced dead."

With deliberate steps, Jack pulls a bottle of Scotch from the top shelf of a kitchen cabinet. After one swallow and another, he takes the bottle with him to the living room. An hour later, numbed by alcohol and despair, he curls up on the couch. With his arms wrapped around his torso, he drifts into an exhausted sleep. Repetitive nightmares soon beset him. In his dreams, he runs as fast as he can to save his children, but he's too late, always.

A few minutes before sunrise, Jack awakens to the sound of his children's laughter. Months before, he had recorded them laughing and installed the taped voices as his alarm ringtone. He sits up, stretches, and then recoils when memories of the accident assault him anew. Terror seizes his heart and, wide-eyed, Jack stares at the family photo on the fireplace mantle. The agony of what happened the day before returns. Instead of going for his daily run, the distraught man dresses and leaves for the hospital.

INTENSIVE CARE

The elevator comes to a stop with a high-pitched whine. Jack braces himself and steps out into the bright hallway light. Tapping his fingers against his thigh, he swallows his apprehension and takes unsure steps toward the Neuro-Intensive Care area. Doctors, nurses, and other medical staff rush in and out of the sliding doors. He stands alone against the corridor wall and tries to make sense of it all. No one seems to notice him—not even the phlebotomist pushing a cart past him.

Jack shifts into the path of a nurse and blurts, "Can you help me? My wife is in there, and I'd like to be with her."

"I can try. What's her name?"

"Sarah. Sarah Jameson. She was admitted late yesterday. Auto accident."

Compassionately, the nurse focuses on Jack and touches his arm. "Mr. Jameson, your wife hasn't regained consciousness. Because of the precariousness of her situation, she cannot have visitors. You should have been told that. I'll let the team know you're here and will ask if one of the doctors can speak with you."

Jack hangs his head and draws in his lower lip. "I'd appreciate that."

"It's best you move into the waiting room. This hallway is a busy place. You understand, right?"

"Yes, ma'am. I don't want to be in the way."

"Your wife is much loved, Mr. Jameson. She's in good hands. I'll tell the team you're here."

The nurse walks through the double doors that hide Sarah and others who have a tenuous hold on life. Whiffs of antiseptics float past Jack and threaten his already unsettled belly. Sucker-punched by the surrealness of it all, he moves into the waiting area and collapses into a steel-framed armchair. Though alone, the place pulses with the fears left behind by unknown others worried for their loved ones.

Glassy-eyed, Jack crosses his arms and rubs his limbs rhythmically. Suddenly, a flashback transports him to Afghanistan.

M16 bullets shish past him and spray the area with deadly force. He sees his friend, Jimmy, get hit. After rushing to his side, he tries to save him. "I've got you," Jack cries out. "I've got you. Hang on!" He throws the Marine over his shoulder and carries him to the medics. Adrenaline surges through his body as he tries to save his friend. The medics work quickly but there is little they can do. "It's too late, sir. We've lost him."

Jack pants through the memory of what he doesn't want to recall. Haunted by the past, Jack wrings his hands and stands to look out the window.

Dr. Roberts enters the room. "Ahem . . . Jack."

"Yes?" He spins around and meets the surgeon. Concern darkens the doctor's eyes, and Jack braces for the worst.

"Your wife survived the night, which is promising, but her condition remains critical. I cannot make any promises about what lies ahead."

"But, but . . . I haven't told her I love her. We tell each other every day."

Dr. Roberts grimaces and sighs. "She's not conscious and doesn't appear like herself. I don't know what she can hear but suspect nothing. I'll hold the door open to her room so you can see her. That's the best I can do. Maybe heart-to-heart is the way to tell her that you love her."

Jack nods. "Okay, I can do that." He wipes tears from his eyes and follows the doctor.

Roberts leads the tormented man to a spot a few feet from the door.

"You can stand here, but you must stay quiet. Whisper or speak only with your heart."

Jack's chin quivers as he squints in search of Sarah. Upon seeing the unmoving mound on the bed, his eyes widen. Tubes, machines, monitors, and pneumatic devices beep and hum, and hide Sarah from him. Her head is wrapped, and Jack can barely make out the contours of her features. She is swollen beyond recognition.

Dr. Roberts recognizes his confusion and puts his hand on Jack's shoulder. "Talk with your heart, son. If anyone can reach her, you can."

Jack bows his head and closes his eyes. With his face contorted in anguish, he prays as he's never prayed before, *Dear God, take my life, not Sarah's. She still has so much to give. Restore her to health, I pray. I'm here, take me.* After a few more minutes, he exhales and gazes at the neurosurgeon. "What should I do?"

Dr. Roberts's eyes soften. "There's not much you can do. She's in God's hands. Do you have family nearby?"

"Yes."

"I think some time with them would be good."

"It . . . it's possible they're at the house now."

"Go join them. There's nothing you can do here. Come back this evening, and I'll update you on your wife's progress."

Jack rubs his hands together and grasps for words. "Okay. I'll do that."

"Do you know a minister or priest?"

"I know the minister who baptized my children."

"You might want to visit him or her."

After clearing his throat, Jack thanks the surgeon and doubles back to the waiting room to fetch his frayed black baseball cap. Five years prior, Sarah had surprised him with this hat and a ticket to a Diamondback game. A smile stretches across his face when he remembers that moment.

The cap sits on the windowsill. As he reaches for it, a crow lands on the outside ledge, and again, Jack's sucked into a time warp. *In Afghanistan, he advances with his platoon through a decimated village. Several crows feast on spilled wheat, a few feet away from a slaughtered family. Jack recoils at the smell of blood and the horror of the Taliban's vengeance and yells at his team to stay vigilant. Then comes the call, IED!*

Jack's cell rings and shocks him back to the present. With pupils dilated, he breathes heavily and turns around, confused. Finally, he realizes he's in the hospital.

Mouth agape, he picks up his phone. "Hello?"

"Where are you, Jack?" His sister says.

"The hospital. I'm leaving now. I'll be at the house in ten."

CHAPTER 5

TELLING THE FAMILY

Jack shuffles to his home, walks past his sister's Subaru in the driveway, and climbs the steps to the front door. Chrissy, a feisty 24-year-old with ash blond hair and a pixie cut, spots her brother through the window and rushes to meet him. She throws her arms around Jack and holds him longer than usual.

"You're white as a sheet, bro. Tell me what's going on. You can count on me for anything and everything."

Jack whispers, "Thank you," and once inside, he collapses onto the couch.

Chrissy cuddles next to him and takes his hand. "How is she?"

Jack sighs and gazes blankly at nothing in particular. "Not good. I couldn't see her, just a peek from the corridor."

"Did you talk with the doctor?"

"Yeah, but he didn't say much. Sarah's not conscious and remains on life-support." Jack pauses. "He said we have to wait."

Chrissy lays her head on his shoulder. "Tell me what I can do to help, and consider it done."

Jack rubs his thighs and turns, wet-eyed, to his sister. "The coroner left a message. The babies are ready for transfer. I don't know what to do."

"I'll take care of it. I know a few folks at the local funeral home. I'll call them and make the arrangements."

"Shouldn't we wait for Sarah?"

"Did the surgeon indicate when she might awaken?"

His face contorts and Jack shakes his head.

Chrissy tightens her hold on her brother's hand. "We need to proceed. Sarah would want the children laid to rest. Don't you agree?"

At his nod, she says, "Do you have a family plot?"

"Plot? No. Who plans for something like this, other than old people?"

"Shall we go to the cemetery together and find a place? Maybe near Mom and Dad?"

"I can't think about it right now. Can you, please, take care of it?"

"Of course. Have you called Sarah's parents?"

Jack flinches and looks at Chrissy with desperation. "No. I, ah, I didn't think to do that. Everything's moved so fast. I, ah . . ."

Chrissy grabs his arm. "Stop. It's not too late. What's the number? I'll take care of it."

Jack reaches into his pocket and pulls out his cell. After scrolling through his contacts, he shows Chrissy the number and listens while she makes the call. He hears Sarah's mother scream and recoils at her reaction. Pushing up from the couch, Jack plods stone-faced out the back door, where he sits on the steps, head in his hands. Back at the scene of the accident, he kneels by his babies and chokes back his hot tears as the rage percolates. Distracted, he runs his hands through his thick mane, and struggles for composure.

Chrissy finishes the call and joins Jack on the steps. She glances at her brother and wraps her arm around his back.

With his stare fixed on his yard, Jack mumbles, "I need to mend the picket fence. Half the posts are leaning or rotten or missing."

"What? That can wait, bro. There's—"

"See over there?" He points to a collapsed post in the north corner. "What a mess. Maybe I should start there."

"Jack. I've something important to discuss."

He side-glances at her.

"Sarah's parents asked if the babies could be buried in their family plot."

Jack makes no response.

Chrissy stretches to peer into Jack's eyes. "I told them I'd talk with you."

"Do whatever."

"They'd like a Christian burial."

"Please, just handle it. But no wake, no reporters. Only family."

"I'll take care of it." His sister stands and strokes his head, "You'll get through this. You will."

Chrissy calls Sarah's mother and explains Jack's wishes. After she hangs up, she joins Jack as he walks the borders of the backyard.

"Everything's taken care of, bro."

"What do you mean?"

"Sarah's mom will handle the arrangements. She's agreed to limit it to family and no wake."

Vacantly, Jack stares at his yard and says, "There's one more thing, sis."

"What?"

"The coroner told me I need a personal injury lawyer."

"You'd like me to handle it?"

"Please. I can't think straight. One minute I'm in Afghanistan, the next I'm at the accident. My head's messed up."

"Stress does that to people, Jack. Not just you. I'll follow up with the personal injury attorney. My friends may know someone, and maybe Mom or Dad have a recommendation. Whatever, I'll find someone good."

CHAPTER 6

THE FUNERAL

The following week, Jack and Chrissy get into his navy-blue pickup to drive across town to the cemetery.

"When did you get the truck?"

"It's a rental. Dad called the insurance company yesterday and arranged for it."

"The old man loves you, Jack."

"I know."

"Are you ready for the burial?"

"Is anyone ever ready?" His hands tighten on the steering wheel. "I'm not sure I can do this."

"You can. Stand next to me. We'll face it together."

Jack drives through the graveyard entrance and pauses. "Where do I turn?"

"The plot is in the Catholic section—a few feet ahead of us and to the right." Chrissy points. "Isn't that Dad's SUV?"

"Yeah. I'll park near him." Jack makes a quick turn and parallel parks behind his father's car.

Once out of the vehicle, he asks Chrissy if he looks presentable.

"Really?" She gives him an impish grin. "Well, using a comb a couple of times a day would help." She pulls a comb from her purse and gives it to him. After a few run-throughs, he hands it back.

"When's the last time you shaved?"

"I don't know. I've lost track of time."

"Well, bro, I'll get you on schedule. Folks will excuse you today, but you need some major time in front of a mirror."

Jack gives her a little shove. "You've made your point. What about my clothes?"

"As I said, you've got an excuse today."

Together, the siblings follow the cracked cement pathway, which leads to the burial site, and stand beside their parents. Jack scans the scene and spots Sarah's mom and dad. They sit on a resting bench under a shade tree that faces the large family headstone. To the right of the monument lies a small grave marker with two little angels engraved on its surface, ready to be placed after the ceremony.

"I can't do this," Jack whispers to his sister and tries to pull away.

Chrissy squeezes Jack's hand. "Of course, you can. You stood for your brother Marines. You can stand for your babies."

Jack's father moves closer to his son, and quietly but firmly says, "There are times when we do what we must, even if we don't want to. This is one of those moments."

Jack fights his angry tears and clenches his jaw. Then he exhales and nods his agreement.

Sarah's mother wipes her tears and rushes to Jack. Crying her words, she expresses her sorrow. He pats her back but wants to run away, far away. The officiating priest recognizes Jack's distress and calls the mourners together. He begins with a prayer and motions for the funeral servers to bring the tiny coffins. The pallbearers proceed into the gathering and set the precious remains in front of the stone marker with the two angels.

At the priest's direction, everyone bows their heads. Jack doesn't hear what the minister says. His attention travels to a distant lawnmower and a yellow butterfly resting on the spray of flowers. Chrissy notices his distraction and gives him a shoulder shove, which jolts him back to the horror of the moment.

Jack straightens and curls his fingers into fists. *Nothing seems real. But it is. Why can't I feel anything? I'm alive, but I wish I weren't.*

Chrissy whispers, "You've got to greet those who've come to show their respects."

He shakes his head in defiance.

"You must. That's absolute. I'll stand next to you. When they come by, say *thank you.* That's all—*thank you.*"

He pulls out his sorrow-filled handkerchief and wipes his tears. Then, standing erect, his shoulders squared, he acknowledges the mourners who pass by to offer their regrets. Jack thought he might feel something, but he doesn't. Numbness has stolen his heart.

"I . . . I've got to get back to the hospital, sis. Sorry, but I've got to go." With those few words, Jack darts to the pickup, and Chrissy chases after him. She jumps into the passenger seat as he turns the ignition key. Breathing heavily, he snaps, "I've got to get out of here. I can't breathe. It's like there's a boulder on my chest." And with that, he jerks away from the curb and swerves through the streets, ignoring his sister's shouts to slow down. Once he pulls into his driveway, Jack skids to a stop.

Chrissy yells, "You could have killed someone—me for example."

Jack climbs out of the truck and slams the door. Without saying a word, he marches down the street and toward the hospital.

Chrissy calls out, "I'm talking to you. What's going on in your dense head?"

Jack offers a wave but never looks back.

"Sheesh, you could at least say goodbye or thank you."

Without turning around, Jack shouts, "Goodbye," and cuts across the busy street to the sound of irritated drivers honking and brakes screeching.

CHAPTER 7

WORRIES FOR JACK

Chrissy watches her brother stride down the street. With his head hung low and shoulders hunched, he seems unaware of traffic and deaf to random hellos. She surveys the neighborhood and observes a man in his front yard with a rake in his hand. His eyes focus on Jack. At that moment she realizes she's not the only one who feels concern. *I've got to help him get back on track. He's as bad as he was when he was first discharged from the service.*

Her cell phone rings and captures the neighbor's attention. Chrissy waves to the man and answers the phone.

"Mom?"

"Are you free to talk?"

"Yeah. Jack took off to the hospital a few minutes ago. I'm at his house. I plan to take the day to clean it."

"I've called him a few times, but he won't pick up."

"Don't take it personally, Mom. He's not himself. Sometimes he thinks he's in Afghanistan."

"Oh, God, should I come over?"

"I don't think so. He needs to figure this out on his own."

"Your dad and I are worried. It's hard to get even two words out of him."

"Yeah, I know. I'm scared as well. I keep praying for a breakthrough—something to help him get beyond the immediate."

"What about Pastor Davis? Do you think Jack would talk with him?"

"Doubt it. He barely manages to converse with strangers. To talk with someone he knows might push him over the edge."

"What edge?"

"I'm not sure. I'm no psychologist, but he needs space. I'll do the laundry, pick up whatever messes are around, and try to make the house feel safe for him. It doesn't now—too many memories. He rehearses the accident over and over again and blames himself for what happened."

"Why would he do that? He wasn't driving."

"I know, but he believes he should have been."

Their worried mother sighs deeply. "Call me whenever, dear, and count on me for anything. I mean that—anything."

"There is one thing."

"What's that?"

"Jack's been advised to work with a personal injury lawyer, and he . . . well . . . he's just not capable at this time."

"I'm on it. This sounds like a great project for your dad. Being a retired cop has its advantages."

Chrissy says her goodbyes and walks up to the house. She pulls a USPS notice from the screen door. It reads, *Your box is full. Going forward, your mail will be held at the Post Office until you notify us that the box is empty.* She shakes her head and mutters, "One more thing to take care of." Chrissy steps into the house and takes the mailbox key from its hook. With a shopping bag in hand, she goes back outside to get Jack's mail. When she tugs open the box door, envelopes cascade out of the postbox. Quickly, Chrissy shoves the sack under the opening and fills it.

Back indoors, she drops the bag of mail on the floor and scans the space. Toys, trucks, superhero figurines, and baby items lay scattered across the floor. Empty beer bottles, soda cans, bags of stale chips, and the remains of frozen dinners lay on and around the couch and cover the coffee table. Chrissy scratches at the back of her neck and speaks out her frustration. "This is a bachelor's pad at its worst. Totally disgusting."

A crumpled blanket on the couch has her exhale slowly, and with compassion, she says, "No wonder he can't think clearly. He's not sleeping."

With jaw set and lips puckered, she pushes up her sleeves and begins the clean-up.

In the kitchen, she empties random coffee cups into the sink and opens the dishwasher, only to discover it's full. "I should have expected that," she groans. Chrissy reaches below the sink for soap and finds there is none. "Oh, course not!" She pulls a pencil and paper from her purse and begins a grocery list.

After she wipes down the countertops, Chrissy pulls out the overflowing trash bag beneath the sink and ties it closed. Then she carries it to the outside barrel at the side of the house. Returning to the kitchen, she grabs the single remaining garbage bag, walks into the living room, and tosses empty bottles, cans, and other trash into the bag, and ties it shut. Another item for her list—trash bags.

Finding the TV remote at the side of the couch, Chrissy speeds through the channels and locates music she likes. Soon, she sings along with Lady Gaga while she cleans. To bring in some natural light, she opens the blinds and lifts the windows for fresh air and cross ventilation. It's then that she notices the goldfish lying on its side.

"Poor thing. I bet you haven't been fed since before the accident." She carries the bowl to the kitchen sink, empties the water, and decides to bury the pet in the backyard. As she walks to the back door, she stumbles over Jack's sneakers. Exasperated, she mumbles, "If it's not one thing, it's another." She sets the shoes on the back doorstep to air out and takes notice of the tall grass and mounds of rotting leaves under the trees.

Several empty beer cans lay at the side of the stoop. She bends to pick them up and a wadded ball of paper under the pile catches her attention. Chrissy sets down the bottles and unravels the scrunched-up paper. It's a love letter to Sarah. She scans the message, *Dearest Sarah . . .* but she pauses at the final three sentences. Chills rush through her as she reads, *I should have been there for you, for the kids. It's my fault. I should be the one in the ground.*

Slowly, Chrissy folds the message and thinks back to when her brother returned from a second tour of duty in Afghanistan. He couldn't sleep and wrote cryptic messages about death. One day she found a suicide note and showed it to their mother, who immediately contacted Veteran's Affairs and got her son professional help. She rubs the side of her face and decides to tell her mom after she finishes cleaning.

Back in the house, Chrissy snags a dirty sweatshirt draped on the arm of an overstuffed chair, picks up the socks and T-shirt on the floor, and heads to the basement. She holds onto the wobbly banister and edges down the wooden steps, unsure of their safety. An earthy-musty whiff of wetness makes her wince. "This place breeds mold."

She spots the washing machine and dryer against the far wall and weaves around old paint cans and scattered boxes to them. She flips open the washer door to find recently washed clothes—now dry. Chrissy exclaims to no one, "Seriously! What have you been doing every night, Jack? Can't put the clothes into the dryer?" She decides to re-wash those clothes and plops the dirty ones she holds onto the cement floor. After searching for the detergent, she moans when she finds an empty box. One more item for the list.

Back upstairs, Chrissy enters the children's candy-striped bedroom. Accidentally, she steps on a crayon and hears Bobby's sweet voice, *Auntie, want to color with me?* She collapses on his little bed and sobs. When she calms, she notices a partially finished bottle of milk next to the rocker and gets back to work.

She strips the sheets from the bed and the crib mattress and tosses other dirty clothes on top of the sheets—the unmatched socks under the bed, the tiny pullovers with cartoon characters, and baby onesies. She carries them all to the basement. Before going back upstairs, she finds an empty box and takes it with her. She piles stuffed animals and squeaky toys into it, lugs the box back downstairs, and adds the collection to the other crates filled with random stuff. She tells herself, *out of sight, out of mind.*

When she revisits the children's room, Chrissy checks the diaper pail and gags. *Of course, it's full.* She pulls out the liner, offers several *phews* at the stench, and takes it to the outside bin.

A glance at her watch shows she needs to go to the grocery store if she plans to finish what she's started. She hops into her car, backs around Jack's pickup, and out of the driveway. Stopped at the intersection, she waits for the light. With a sudden jolt, it dawns on her that she's in the exact location where the babies died. Her head falls with her tears, but the honk of a horn brings her back. Slowly, she proceeds across the intersection.

···✦✦✦···

The late afternoon sun casts shadows throughout the house. Chrissy checks her watch. *It's 5:30 p.m., and Jack ought to be back by now.* She sends him a text. *When are you coming home?*

Not sure.

Shall I wait for you?

No.

Are you okay?

I guess.

Shall I meet you at the hospital?

I'm not there.

Where are you? When she receives no response, she tries again. *Jack, where are you?*

No answer.

Chrissy shouts, "Stupid brother! Do you even care that I've spent the entire day cleaning your house?"

She clutches the vacuum cleaner handle and charges after the trails of dirt and crumbs on the frayed carpet—all the while complaining to herself. "Ungrateful brat. Wait till I find him. I'll tell him a thing or two!"

Once she finishes, Chrissy glances about the space and decides it's much better. She takes a few moments to assess the progress. The dishwasher is running, a second load of clothes is washing, and the dryer is pounding. She pats herself on the back, *Things are shaping up.*

As a final gesture, she dumps the bag of mail on the coffee table and announces to no one, "This will give him something to do. As for me, I'm going home."

Chrissy locks the front door, climbs into her SUV, and drives to her parent's house. She strolls in as they sit down to eat.

"Come and join us, honey," her dad says with a side glance. "I know that expression. You wear it when you're frustrated with your brother."

"Don't even get me started. He won't answer my calls. And I've been dealing with his mess all day. It's not right. Who does he think he is?"

"Well," her mother responds, "shall we say Grace?" After getting Chrissy's attention, the woman bows her head and says, "Heavenly Father, we ask for your guidance and mercy. Jack needs help, and we don't know what to do. Open our hearts so that we might hear You. And we thank you for the gifts you've laid before us this evening."

"Amen," Chrissy exclaims. "So, back to Jack."

"I know you're worked up, dear, but let's eat and chat about pleasanter topics for a bit."

"Like what? Really."

Her dad clears his throat and answers back, "Like . . . this roast is amazing."

"All right, I get it, but your son, *my brother*, is going off the deep end."

"What the hell do you mean by that?"

"He's in between worlds, Dad. Sometimes he's in Afghanistan, then he's at the accident, then he's back in the trenches. I'm telling you, he can't think right. He's a prisoner of his mind. Who knows where he is now? I wouldn't be surprised if he's lost somewhere, wandering around like a madman."

Her mother and father exchange glances. "We'll stop by this evening and check on him."

"You guys baby him." Chrissy crosses her arms.

Her dad responds with firmness, "Enough. Just because you're upset with your brother, you don't have the right to speak to us like that. We'll go visit him after dinner. Let's move on to other topics."

··•◆•··

Later that evening, Mr. Jameson grabs his keys and motions to his wife. "Let's go find Jack."

"It's probably not as bad as Chrissy says. You know how she can exaggerate."

"One way or another, we must find out. If he's experiencing post-traumatic stress symptoms again, we need to step in."

Thirty minutes later, the worried father pulls into the driveway. The house stands dark.

"This isn't good. It looks like no one's home."

"Maybe he went to bed already."

"Really? It's seven-thirty. Have you ever known him to go to bed that early?"

"No, you're right. This doesn't look good."

The concerned parents walk up to the door and ring the bell—several times. There's no response.

"I'll go around the back. You stay here." Jack's father hobbles to the rear entrance and pounds on the door.

From the other side of the fence, a neighbor calls out, "Hello?" Mr. Jameson jumps in surprise.

"Sir, name's Fred. I haven't seen Jack all day. When he gets home in the evening, he likes to sit on the back steps and have a cold one. That's when we chat. I think he still must be at the hospital."

"Thanks for letting me know. I'm his father. I, ah, hoped to talk with him."

"I understand. If I see him, I'll be sure to tell him that you came by. Sad situation."

"Couldn't agree more. Thanks for everything."

After limping back to the front, he calls out to his wife, "Let's get out of here. Who knows when he'll be back."

"Maybe we could visit tomorrow. Perhaps a little earlier and bring him dinner."

Jack's father knuckles down on the steering wheel, engrossed in his concerns. "What was that?"

"We could bring him dinner tomorrow."

"Sounds good."

CHAPTER 8

THE DECISION

Jack paces the hallway near his wife's hospital room. While scrubbing his hand over his face, he swears under his breath. *It's been four days. Four days since the funeral. I should have answers!* The ticking of the corridor clock pounds in his head. His eyes narrow as he plots how he'll destroy that noisy beast. The elevator doors open with a rumble, and Jack pivots and exclaims, "Thank God. Dr. Roberts."

He rushes to the doctor's side and asks the question that is ever present in his thoughts, "Doctor, please, just a moment. I need to know—what are the odds Sarah will awaken? Please be honest with me."

The surgeon studies Jack intently and cocks his head upward. He chooses his words carefully. "I can't give you the odds, Jack, but the facts are that each passing day is another day lost. I've witnessed patients awakening after three weeks, a few after four, but more than that . . . well, it's rare."

Jack pulls his fingers through his disheveled mop and squeezes his eyes shut to process the information. "I buried my babies last week. I don't know if I can face burying Sarah as well." He turns and stares blankly at the doctor.

"I wish I could give you better news. All I can say is we're doing everything we can to save your wife."

Jack draws in a breath and releases it. "Thank you for being frank." He focuses on the doors that hold his wife captive. "Can I visit her?"

The surgeon nods. "Yes, but remember, only for a few minutes. She's off the ventilator but still hasn't regained consciousness. Talk with her as though she stands in front of you. It may help."

With mounting apprehension, Jack approaches his comatose wife. He picks up her limp hand and laces her fingers inside his. Then, kissing her forehead, he whispers, "Soon, I will be with you, my love."

Dr. Roberts checks his watch and motions for Jack to leave. With reluctance, the distraught husband follows him out of the room.

"Thank you for giving me this final moment with her."

"There's no need to assume it's a final moment, Jack. I'm still hopeful."

Jack rolls his shoulders and says goodbye.

With robotic precision, Jack marches out of the hospital and down the street to his home. He hears a few *hellos* from neighbors, but his thoughts remain with the words of the doctor. *I've witnessed patients awakening after three weeks, a few after four, but more than that, it's rare.* He yanks open the door, enters, and slams it shut.

What's the use? The babies are gone. Sarah probably won't make it. Who am I without them? I can't attend another funeral . . . unless . . . unless it's mine.

Jack locks his jaw and, with determination, struts into his bedroom. He opens the closet and reaches for a small safe on the shelf. He unlocks it and pulls out his revolver. After grasping a handful of ammunition, he slams its door shut.

He tilts his head upward, puckers his lips, and stomps back into the living room.

Then he spots the pile of unopened mail on the coffee table and yells his frustration. He swipes his arm across the surface, and the envelopes go flying. Slump-shouldered, Jack drops down onto the couch and scans the space. It's been wiped clean of life. He blinks away tears and tightens his jaw. Fingering his weapon, Jack releases the cylinder and loads two shells. Then he leans into the couch cushions and considers the aim. After pulling back the hammer, he rests his eyes on the family photo propped on the fireplace.

The doorbell rings, and Jack freezes. It rings again, and his father calls his name. Jack doesn't move. His mother says, "He must be at the hospital. Let's leave the box and visit tomorrow." Jack waits for them to leave, and upon hearing their car back out of the driveway, he refocuses on the grim task. He raises his weapon and gives the space a final once-over. An envelope with several foreign stamps lies on the floor, atop the pile of scattered mail.

Curious, Jack puts down his weapon and picks up the letter. It's from Mateo Silva, his college friend and fellow Marine. *Why did he write to me? He couldn't have known about the accident.* Jack tears open the envelope and finds it's not what he expected.

Hey Jack,

I've been thinking of you. Don't know why. Maybe because we spent so much time together. If you haven't heard, Susan and I split up. Not a pretty scene. I walked away with nothing but my hiking boots, sleeping bag, and some clothes. Took it as an omen and decided to take the trip I'd wanted to take for years.

I just got off the train in Saint Jean Pied de Port. Yep, I'm starting the French Way of the El Camino de Santiago. I'm at a local café, standing at the bar with other caffeine-desperate folks, sipping my coffee. I've got to figure out my next steps and why not do it on a pilgrimage? That's why I'm writing.

How about joining me? Maybe your sister could help Sarah with the kids. I suspect I'll reach Burgos, Spain, in ten days. That would be a great place for us to rendezvous. I plan on spending a few days in that location to explore the local culture and cuisine. Supposedly, they have wineries to die for, and you know I love good wine.

Here's my proposal. I've got a bed in a hostel close to the cathedral. I'll wander over to the church plaza every evening and check for you, in case you've taken the leap. I'll be the one with a wine glass in hand.

Maybe you think me crazy for making this trip. Maybe I would have thought the same a few years back. It took hell to bring me to my knees. This past year topped Afghanistan in pure torture. I figure, what do I have to lose? Who even cares about me? Maybe something freaky will happen on this trip. Who knows, maybe I'll find God. If I do, I've got a long list of questions.

As I mentioned, you've been on my mind. Whether you make the trip or not, let's get together soon.

All the best to Sarah and the kids,

Mateo

Fixedly, Jack stares at the letter and then surveys the room that once held playthings and evidence of family activity. A ghoulish thought grips his heart, and he picks up his revolver. After cocking the hammer again, he points it under his jaw and angles it toward his skull. He closes his eyes. Just as Jack touches the trigger, he hears his Captain's voice and freezes. *Snap out of it, Marine. Man up! It's time for you to find a reason to live.*

Ashen, Jack's lips tremble. "Ca-Captain?" He stutters but can't find the words. "Are you here?" He turns to check the room but sees no one. With a shaky hand, he sets the gun on the coffee table and says aloud, "I've got to find Matt. He's my only hope."

Unruly beads of sweat gather on Jack's forehead. He needs to get to Burgos. He checks the date, *I've at least four days to get there and find him.* Jack disarms his weapon, goes back into the bedroom, and puts the gun into the safe. Then he heads down to the basement and sweeps the area for his old college storage trunk. He finds it under a pile of Christmas decorations. Jack drags the container into the center of the crowded space, pulls out coats and mementos, and locates what he's searching for: his boots, a collapsible trekking pole, rain gear, and his backpack.

Once upstairs with his gear, Jack calls a travel agent and arranges a flight to Madrid and a train to Burgos. Then he stuffs his pack with a few T-shirts and an extra pair of jeans. He grabs his cap, sets his phone on the counter, and walks out onto the stoop. At his feet sits a boxed meal. He peeks at the tag, *Love, Mom,* and pockets the soda can and the cookies.

Then, after slamming the door shut, he gets into the rental pickup and heads to the Phoenix Sky Harbor International Airport.

···✦✦✦···

Across the town, Jack's father paces back and forth in his den. "I'm worried, Louise. It's like a repeat of when he got back from the war. This isn't good. We've got to do something."

"I'm worried too, Sam." She bites her nails and glances at him pleadingly. "He's withdrawn from everyone. No one knows where he is. He doesn't answer our phone calls. He's not at his house or doesn't come to the door. What are we supposed to do?"

Sam releases a deep sigh. "We need to get Chrissy's help."

"You know what she'll say."

"Yeah. But she's the only one who can find him. The two are like night and day, but they care about and protect each other." He stares down at his cell phone and tightens his lips. "I'm calling."

"Dad?"

"Yep, it's me. I need your assistance. I'd like you to help us find Jack. It's been two days and no word."

"Are you admitting there's a problem?"

With a sigh, her father replies, "Yes. You were right and we were wrong. So, will you help?"

"Yeah, of course. I don't like being my brother's keeper, but I love the jerk, so I'll do what I can."

"Thank you. Get back to us as soon as you know anything. Okay?"

"It's a deal."

···✦✦✦···

Chrissy smiles mischievously. *Dad doesn't often admit he's wrong. They must be worried. I'll find Jack for them.* She speed-dials her brother and shouts to no one. "Give me a break, Jack! Why don't you answer your phone?" Chrissy waits until the call goes to voicemail and exclaims, "It's your sister—AGAIN—where are you? Mom and Dad are worried." She gives the phone her best evil eye and shouts, "AAARRRGHH!"

Chrissy pinches her lips together and decides to drive to his house before it gets too late. Her parents are unaware she's privy to the location of a duplicate key. After jumping into her car, she grips the steering wheel like she's racing in the Grand Prix and, scrunching her face, she says loudly, "Why do I bother—or care? He doesn't even return my calls. Didn't even say *thank you* after I worked so hard to clean up his mess. Well, I'll tell him a thing or two. This has got to end." She turns onto his driveway and comes to an abrupt stop. Jack's truck is gone.

Chrissy gets out of her SUV, stomps to the front door, and pushes the doorbell. No one answers. "Of course, there's no answer. Even if you're inside, you wouldn't bother, would you, Jack?" Frustrated, she goes around to the back, finds the extra key under the porch, and returns to unlock the front door. Just as she starts to enter the house, she notices a box plopped on its side by the stoop and bends to check it out.

"Yuck! Animals have eaten whatever was in this thing." Then she reads the tag, *Love, Mom,* and smirks. "As I said, they baby him."

Once inside, Chrissy calls out but hears no reply. She scans the place and thinks out loud, "Hmm, basically decent, except for the letters scattered on the floor." When Chrissy twists around, she finds Jack's phone on the counter. "That's strange. Why would he leave his phone, aside from not wanting to listen to my messages?" She checks the sink. "As I suspected, dirty dishes. Some things never change." Then, entering his bedroom, she sees his dresser drawers stand ajar and the clothes in them lie in disarray, as though her brother were looking for something in a hurry. She knits her brows and crosses her arms. "He's flown the coop."

CHAPTER 9

THE AWAKENING

The early morning sun sends shafts of light through the windows in Sarah's private hospital room. Nurses move in and out, checking her vital signs and recording the findings. Body temperature, pulse rate, respiration rate, and blood pressure. They also adjust her nasal feeding tube. Today, a nurse talks with her as she attends to the morning procedures.

"It's beautiful outside, my friend. From your new room, you can look out to Red Rock Park. You'll love the view once you're awake. I've been thinking about a stroll along the water's edge. Our city may not have a beach, but we've beautiful lakes. Do you remember when we packed a bag lunch and went to Tabaaha Lake on our day off? Kayakers raced across its length. You cheered for one and I for the other. We made a promise to each other that day. Do you remember? We said that someday we would do the same thing—race across the lake." She focuses on the monitor and notes the readings in the log as she continues her monologue. "Let's go have lunch at the lake. What do you think?" She lays her hand on Sarah's. "I miss you, my friend." And at that statement, Sarah's fingers move.

Mouth slackening, the nurse repeats, "I miss you, Sarah." Again, she feels the fingers lift. "Oh my gosh. Oh my gosh," she shouts. Then, more calmly, she says, "Can you open your eyes, my dear?" She studies Sarah's visage and perceives movement around the eyelids. "Sarah, try to open your eyes." The nurse waits and entreats, "Try to . . ." Then it happens. Sarah's eyes flutter open.

"I'm calling the doctor right now." The nurse speaks rapidly into her phone, "Dr. Roberts, Sarah is awake."

Within minutes, the surgeon rushes into the restricted area and to his patient's bedside.

"Sarah, welcome back." He takes Sarah's hand and speaks slowly, "You're in the hospital. You had an accident and took a hard blow to the head." He observes her and notes that Sarah's eyes move side to side. He pushes a button and raises the head of the bed slowly, so she can see better.

Sarah moves her lips, but no sound emerges.

The doctor moves closer to her and says, "Please say it again. I couldn't hear you."

Sarah utters two barely audible words, "My babies."

Dr. Roberts steps back and takes a deep breath. Then he rests his hand on hers and leans closer. With tenderness, he peers into her unfocused eyes and delivers the horrifying news.

"No. That can't be. I saw them."

"They play with angels now, Sarah."

When Sarah finally grasps what the doctor means, she cries out. Her wail echoes across the room, and the doctor gulps down his resolve.

After she regains composure, she whispers, "My husband."

Dr. Roberts glances over at the nurse and back to Sarah. "You've been in a coma for a couple of weeks. Your husband sat at your side every day, but he isn't here today. Perhaps he's gone back to work."

Sarah's eyes water and tears fall down her cheeks. "So sad."

"It is, but today I'm happy, and Jack will be elated when he learns you're awake." The doctor squeezes her hand. "I'll check for sensation. Let's start with your toes."

Methodically, the surgeon checks her reflexes while the nurse chronicles each response. "Can you move your toes for me?"

"I, ah, I don't know."

"Try. Concentrate on your toes and nothing else. Tell them to move." When he detects movement, the doctor beams. "We're in business. Now, try to lift your foot. Again, think only about lifting your foot."

Sarah furrows her brow and closes her eyes. Slowly, her foot rises.

The nurse wipes away tears as the doctor struggles to contain his excitement. "Let's check if you can lift your leg. Remember, pay attention only to your leg."

Sarah squints her eyes and takes a deep breath. "Uhh," she groans. Her leg moves.

Dr. Roberts turns to the nurse and tells her to call physical therapy to arrange for progressive therapy ASAP and schedule a brain scan. Then he adds, "Call her husband. Let him know Sarah is awake. If you can't reach him, call whoever is listed as next of kin."

"I'm on it," the nurse responds and hurries to the nurses' station.

The surgeon elevates the head of the bed higher, so Sarah achieves a sitting position, and then checks the monitors for any sign of stress. None show. In disbelief, he says, "It's a miracle, Sarah. It's almost as though you were asleep these last weeks. Your blood oxygen levels are good, your lungs are clear, and your eyes aren't dilated. The only visible damage is the bruising along the left side of your body. We have a few more tests to do, but I couldn't have imagined a more positive outcome than this. I believe you're going to be okay."

Sarah struggles with tears and whispers, "I'm overwhelmed. Could you do one thing for me?"

"Certainly."

"Could I speak with a chaplain?"

"I'll make sure he or she visits you today."

·· + ◆ + ··

Down the hallway, the nurse arranges the appointments for Sarah and then calls Jack. Since there's no response, she calls the next of kin—Chrissy Jameson.

Chrissy works at the Parks and Recreation Center as both manager and instructor. Her yoga class begins in a few minutes. As the students arrive and claim their spot on the floor, she welcomes them. Upon hearing her phone, she reaches to silence it but sees County Central Hospital flash on the screen. "I've got to take this call," she says to her class.

Chrissy moves out of hearing range of her students and answers the phone. "Hello, Chrissy here."

"Ms. Jameson, I couldn't reach Jack, and you are listed as next of kin."

"What's wrong?"

"It's not what's wrong; it's what's right. Sarah Jameson is awake and appears to be doing well."

"Oh my God, can I visit her?"

"Early evening would be best. The surgeon has ordered a full assessment, and that will take most of the afternoon."

"Thank you for letting me know. I'll come straight from work—about six."

Chrissy disconnects, makes a quick call to her parents and to Sarah's, then circles back to her class. She apologizes for the interruption and explains, "Miracles happen, my friends. That was a call from the hospital. My dear sister-in-law just awakened from a coma after nearly three weeks. She's a living miracle—as are you. Let's celebrate and stretch and breathe in thanksgiving."

CHAPTER 10

THE AGREEMENT

Sarah stares out the windows that overlook the park and dozes in and out of sleep. Other than nurses visiting regularly to check on her progress, her room is quiet.

A tall, dark-skinned woman with short white hair walks into the room and greets Sarah. The new voice rouses her.

"Hello, Mrs. Jameson, I'm Georgina Rustin, one of the ministers at Holy Cross Church. I volunteer at the hospital two days a week. Dr. Roberts called and asked me to meet with you."

With a faltering voice, Sarah says, "Thank you for coming. I told him I'd like to speak with a chaplain. I'm glad you could spare the time."

"It's always a pleasure, my dear. Let's begin with a short prayer and then chat, okay?"

"Yes, I'd like that very much."

The chaplain bows her head and closes her eyes. "God of all creation, You who love each of us and accompany us through our struggles, be with Sarah and me today. Bless us as we talk and help us better understand your Divine will. With gratitude, we pray. And so, it is." She looks over at Sarah and smiles, "How can I help you, my dear?"

"I, ah, I've been in a coma for a few weeks, so I'm a little befuddled. I was in a terrible car accident, and my two little children did not survive. What I want to share is what occurred when I had surgery."

"Anything you say to me is confidential, Sarah, so please speak freely."

"Something happened on the operating table."

"Yes?"

"I died and floated above everyone. I watched as Dr. Roberts tried to save me. I could hear and see everything. I even saw him call the time of death. But I neither felt pain nor fear. I only felt peace—and curiosity. I tried to reach the team, to tell them not to worry, but they couldn't hear me. Then I traveled away from the surgical ward—away from everyone. Suddenly, I found myself in a beautiful garden with lots of flowers, and that's where I saw my children. They played happily, and when they saw me, they waved and giggled. They were so joyous, and so was I.

"Then an angel, at least I'm calling her an angel, approached me. She explained I had a choice—to remain with my kids or to return to my husband, Jack. I wanted to stay with my babies. I was so happy in that garden with them. But I saw Jack sitting in the waiting room. I saw his tears, and I felt his tortured heart. I realized how alone he was, and that is when I decided I had to return to this earthly life. I couldn't leave him in such a state."

Sarah pauses and gazes at the minister. "Does this make sense to you?"

"Yes, and you're not the only one who's had this experience. I've listened to similar stories from others who experienced clinical death."

"I didn't know if I should tell Dr. Roberts or not. I don't want him to think I'm unstable."

"He's a neurosurgeon, right?"

"Yes."

"I'm sure other patients have shared comparable experiences with him. Why do you want to tell him?"

"I saw how much he cared, and how protective he is of his team. He went the extra mile for me and didn't give up. I want to thank him."

Georgina reaches for Sarah's hand. "Even if he questions your experience, which I sincerely doubt, gratitude is a universal virtue. Who doesn't appreciate a sincere *thank you?*"

A quick knock at the door, and a hearty *hello*, prompts both women to focus on the doorway, where Dr. Roberts stands.

"Oh my, two of my favorite people. Chaplain Georgina, nice to see you again. And Sarah, how are you doing?"

"I'm feeling better, Doctor. And the chaplain and I have had a wonderful conversation."

The chaplain pats Sarah's hand and responds to Dr. Roberts. "It's nice to see you as well. Thank you for inviting me to meet with Sarah. It's been a pleasure, and I hope we'll talk again soon. I will go now so that you two can chat privately. I've several more patients to visit. Good day to you both." Georgina gets up to leave and says to Sarah, "Remember, I'm here for you. You can ask to speak with me anytime."

Dr. Roberts gives Sarah a thumbs up. "It sounds like you've got a new friend."

"She's so kind, and I'd like to think of her as a friend."

The surgeon picks up the medical chart and checks Sarah's vitals. "Everything looks good. I'm still surprised by the readings. Some things are unexplainable." He walks to the end of her bed to check her reflexes. His poker face lights up. "Has the physical therapist visited you yet?"

"Not that I'm aware of, but I've dozed on and off."

"I'll give him another call. You need to start moving. Otherwise, how are things?"

"Good, I think. I feel like I've been gone for a long time, and it's a perplexing sensation."

"Tomorrow, you'll feel more settled. Your body is still waking up, so there's no need to worry."

Sarah wrinkles her brow.

Dr. Roberts asks, "Is everything okay?"

"I think so, but . . ."

"What?"

"There's something I want to tell you."

"I'm here, so let's do it."

"Well, it may sound odd, but here goes. When I died, I saw you trying to revive me. I heard you call the time of death. I saw everyone's despair. But I wasn't in pain or fearful. I felt only peace. I floated above everyone and tried to reassure you, but you couldn't hear me. Then I traveled far away from the surgical ward, through time and space. And I saw my children."

As he listens, Dr. Roberts's eyes widen.

Sarah repeats what she told the chaplain and shares the reason she chose to come back.

"I'm relieved you decided to return. We need you here, Sarah."

"That's kind of you to say. But there's more. I've come to realize we don't really die. We live on in spirit and enter another realm. It's a different life and more real than anything we experience here. But it is life."

Dr. Roberts stares at her. "I don't know how to react to your experience, but I'll share that over my thirty-odd years of neurosurgery, I've listened to several patients talk of another life that awaits." He looks away in thought, then turns back to her. "It will take time and physical therapy to regain your strength, but maybe there's an intermediate step you could take before you resume a full nursing shift."

Sarah meets his gaze with a question, "Something I could do even from a wheelchair?"

"Affirmative, and you'd be offering a great service."

"Please tell me what you're thinking. Without my babies, I'll have a lot of free time." Sarah wipes away a stray tear.

"Well, it's a bit out of the box, but it's something we need. You've worked in the Intensive Care Unit and the Emergency Room, so you understand there's not much time for solace. Medical teams, necessarily, focus on threats to survival. We medicate fear, we don't address it, beyond explaining what we must do."

"And you think I could help with that fear?"

"More or less. You could offer comfort to the comatose and critically ill patients." Dr. Roberts watches her reaction. "You're interested, aren't you?"

"Hmm, what about my physical therapy?"

"Once you're strong enough to meet with patients, I'll make sure we work around your schedule."

"You want me to accompany the dying patients as they take their final steps?"

"Something like that. Many are alone and unresponsive. Maybe if you could share your experience, they'd be more at peace and could decide as you did."

Sarah flushes with tenderness. "It would please me greatly."

CHAPTER 11

THE VISIT

The rattling of the morning food cart stirs Sarah awake. She looks over to the door, expecting to see a server with a tray of food, but instead is surprised to find her parents—George and Clara Wright.

"Mom. Dad," she says in a barely audible voice.

"Darling," her mom says. "We came as soon as we could."

Her father moves to Sarah's side and kisses her forehead. After wiping away a tear, he whispers, "I love you more than life itself. I'm so relieved you're better."

"Though slowly, I'm getting stronger, Dad. Soon I'll be running laps. You'll see."

The worried man exhales a pain-filled breath and holds her hand. "If you only knew."

Her mother interrupts and says, "Sarah, the prayer group at church has been praying for you."

"Please tell them thank you. I'm sure their loving prayers have helped."

"They remember when you attended St. Michael's Church with us."

Sarah flinches at the covert jab but chooses not to respond. Instead, she changes the topic, "Last night Chrissy visited and told me you helped with the funeral and arranged for the babies to be buried in the family plot. I'm incredibly grateful."

Her father glances over at his wife and says, "It was the least we could do."

"I would have arranged for a Mass," her mother says, "but Chrissy said Jack didn't want one. It's customary, you know."

Sarah pinches her lips together. "Mom, I am your only child. All my life, I've tried to please you. Did all the right things—went to church faithfully, helped care for Grandma in her last months, studied hard, and excelled in academics. But nothing was ever good enough. Then when I married the love of my life, you rejected me."

"I didn't reject . . ."

"You shunned me and my family. Be honest with yourself . . . when did you last visit?"

"Well, it wasn't that long ago, was it? I've been . . ."

"Busy? With what, Mom? With what? The last time you saw us was when you stopped by the house to leave Christmas presents. You didn't come in, didn't talk with the kids, and just stood on the stoop and handed me your gifts."

"Well, I thought . . ."

"I know you have excuses. You always have excuses. They're real to you, but to me, they simply say, 'You're not good enough, and I don't have time for you.'"

"That's not true. It's not. Tell her, George. It's not true."

Sarah's father turns away and looks out the window. "It's true."

"How can you say that, George? It's not true. It's about religion, about a difference of belief."

"Say what you will, Clara, but my experience is that you've separated me from the greatest love I've ever known. She lies in front of us, and still, you cannot look her in the eye. I've kept quiet for these past five years, but it's broken my heart. I can't do it anymore."

"What are you saying? She forsook her religion."

"No, she defied your demands that she remain a Catholic. Our beautiful daughter had the audacity to worship in her husband's church. What's wrong with that? Haven't we been taught that God is Love?"

"Of course, but . . ."

"There are no *buts*, Clara. You've set yourself above God. You've done that, and all of us have suffered."

Sarah clears her throat. "Mom, Dad, I've just lost my babies, and I'm still quite weak from the accident. This is a conversation we need to have, but maybe not now. Not here."

George says, "You're right. We'll go."

"Before you do, there's something I need to explain. When I was in surgery, medically I died. I didn't feel pain, and I had no fear. But during that span of time, I saw my children. Bobby and Marci played in a field of beautiful flowers. They were ecstatic. I was with them and shared their bliss. This special place pulsed with love, only love.

"If you care about me genuinely, and want to help, find Jack. He's disappeared, and I'm so worried about him."

Clara shakes her head. "I'm not sure what I can do, but I'll go by the house and . . ."

"Mom, swallow your pride and call Jack's parents. Tell them you want to help and ask them how you can. Even if they say there's nothing you can do, you will have made the effort, and that gesture will go a long way in bridging the differences."

Sarah's father says, "I'll go to your house today. Maybe the yard needs mowing, and if so, I'll handle it. Time is on my side. I've plenty of it, and I'm glad to help. I need to."

"You're an angel, Dad. Thank you."

A nurse walks in and explains that she needs to take Sarah's vitals. When she checks the blood pressure reading, her eyebrows raise. "Umm, your blood pressure is unusually high, Sarah. I'm a little alarmed."

"There's no need. My parents and I had a tough conversation, one we should have had years ago. They'll be leaving in a few minutes. Could you recheck in an hour? I think you'll find I'm back to my normal, 112/70."

After the nurse leaves, Mr. Wright returns to Sarah's side. With eyes downcast and mournful, he grips Sarah's hand. Haltingly, the grieved man says, "Things will change, dear. That is my promise. We'll do our best to find Jack, and we will help you in all the ways we can. We'll be a family again."

CHAPTER 12

THE CEMETERY

A few days after her parents' visit, Sarah leaves the hospital in a wheelchair. Chrissy accompanies her and holds her hand, while an attendant pushes her down the hallway. On either side of the corridor, Sarah's medical team cheers her forward. Teary-eyed, Sarah offers a slight wave and thanks each of them.

The attendant helps Sarah into the waiting SUV. Though a little uncertain of herself, she slides over with ease and fastens the seatbelt. "Thank you for helping me. I appreciate it."

"It's a privilege, Mrs. Jameson. You may not remember my mom, Gina Garcia, but you were the one who gave her hope."

"Gina? I remember her well. She was one of our first COVID patients. How is she doing?"

"Incredibly well. You told her she'd be hiking someday, and she took that comment literally. She walks all the trails in the area. In fact, she's something of a local hero."

"No kidding? Please, give her my love and tell her that, someday, I will join her."

"She'll be happy to hear that." With a quick wave goodbye, he closes the door.

Sarah glances at Chrissy, who sits behind the steering wheel. "Stories like Gina's make all the long hours worth it."

"Brought tears to my eyes, that's for sure. Now let's get you home."

"I can't wait, but if you have the time, could we make another stop first?"

"Of course. I took the day off. Where to?"

"I'd like to visit my babies."

Chrissy takes a deep breath, makes a quick turn onto Hollow Oak Road, and says, "We're on our way." Once merged into the traffic, she glances at Sarah. "You, okay?"

"A couple of days ago my parents visited me, and I thanked them for offering space in their family plot. It gives me a sense of peace to know the little ones rest with family."

"And?"

"Umm, I leveled with Mom. Couldn't help it. It's been a conversation we've needed for a long time."

"About?"

"About church, about Jack."

"And? Come on, no secrets here."

"I said I felt rejected by her. Ever since I married Jack, she's ignored me, the kids, and Jack."

"Heavy stuff."

"Yep, but Dad spoke up and validated what I said."

"Wow. That's extraordinary."

"Time will tell if anything sunk in, but Dad promised me that things would change. He grew tearful during the visit and treated me tenderly."

Chrissy side-glances and says, "Your mom picked out a beautiful granite headstone with two angels engraved on it."

"I'm sure it's lovely. Jack liked it, right?"

"Uh-huh. He was grateful for everything they did."

Sarah gazes out the window for a moment and says, "Maybe the babies are helping our families mend their differences."

"It's possible. At the funeral, your mom embraced Jack and told him how sorry she was."

"For real? That's major. I don't think Mom has spoken to Jack for years. Thank you for letting me know."

"It's paradoxical, but sometimes tragedy brings healing. If it's not a secret, what was your mom so angry about?"

"Truthfully, I don't remember, other than she had strong opinions about where and when little Bobby should be baptized. And, by the way, Mom has strong opinions about a lot of things."

"I kinda got that."

Sarah laughs and says, "I'm so glad we're best friends and in-laws. Which reminds me, I haven't told you about my experience."

"At the accident?"

"In heaven."

"Heaven? No. What are you talking about?"

Sarah exhales slowly and tells her tale for a fourth time.

Chrissy glances at her.

Tears stain Sarah's cheeks.

Stopped at the traffic lights, Chrissy waits and listens.

Sarah says, "An angel gave me a choice—to remain with my babies or come back here. I didn't know what to do, but then I saw Jack and felt his despair. And I couldn't leave him in that state. So, I decided to return for him."

Chrissy brushes aside a tear. "Not a dream?"

"No. When I was alone with Dr. Roberts, I recounted everything that happened in the operating room, including my death. He verified it all and wasn't surprised. He acknowledged he'd heard similar stories."

"I don't know what to say, Sarah. You know me. I'm not exactly the religious type, but your story gives me hope."

"It's all about love, Chrissy. Not magic. Just love. From what I saw, Heaven vibrates with Love."

"What about the bad guys? The drunk who hit you?"

"I don't have any idea as to what happens if a person's heart is closed to Love. But I do know that Love draws us to our eternal home. All of us. I guess a person can refuse Love, but what a horrible thought."

Chrissy clears her throat and changes the subject. She points to a large Juniper tree, slows down, and says, "Your little ones are nearby. I'll pull over to the side and get your wheelchair."

Sarah views the wide expanse of gravestones and arrangements of flowers. A few small flags snap in the breeze. In the distance, a funeral is in progress, and pallbearers carry a casket. When Chrissy opens the door for her to get into the wheelchair, Sarah says matter-of-factly, "Someday, we'll rest here, sis."

"That's a sobering thought. Hopefully, we'll both be ancient when the time comes."

Chrissy pushes the wheelchair past clusters of stone crosses and statues of sun-blanched angels and over to the Catholic section. Sarah asks, "Did Jack mind that the babies were buried in this area?"

"Not at all. He was grateful for your parents' help. Honestly, I don't think he noticed anything, except the headstone for the babies."

After rolling the wheelchair next to the marker, Sarah lays her hand on the granite surface and reads the engraving.

Robert and Marcia Jameson

Ours for a little while

With the angels forever

She stretches forward and kisses the headstone. Then, when she looks around, Sarah sees patches of flowers and notices several goldfinches and white-winged doves. "They're happy, Chrissy. This isn't their home, but they visit to say hello. I can feel their sweet spirits."

"You've always been sensitive to energy and the spirit world. I don't feel anything except this irritating fly that keeps landing on my arm."

"You're hilarious." Sarah takes a deep breath and shifts in her seat. "They didn't suffer. They were spared lengthy hospital treatments and care and, instead, went directly to heaven. They had a peaceful transition."

"Well, that's a nice thought. I hope you're right, but nothing about that day felt peaceful."

"It's a matter of perspective." Sarah smiles at her sister-in-law. "Simply a matter of perspective."

Chrissy wraps her arms around her and asks if she'd like to visit anywhere else.

"Let's go home."

CHAPTER 13

HOME AT LAST

Chrissy turns onto Sarah's driveway and looks, fixedly, at the modest building. With the blinds shut, the lights off, and the cloud cover, it seems as though the house is in mourning.

"Are you ready for this, sis?" Chrissy rubs Sarah's shoulder.

"I don't know if I'll ever be ready, but this is as good a time as ever." She scans the property and remembers *what was* while she observes *what is*. "Someone's taken care of the yard. He or she even tried to fix the leaning posts on the fence. Dad said he'd cut the grass, maybe he's the hero." She wipes a tear and points, "Oh, there's Bobby's tricycle by the garage door. Usually, it lies in the front yard."

Chrissy brings the wheelchair to the passenger door. Carefully, Sarah lifts each leg onto the pavement and holds the door frame while she slides into the chair.

"I can do it from here." Sarah lays her hands on the wheels and rolls toward the door, which now has a ramp that leads up to it. Wide-eyed, she rotates around to Chrissy. "Oh my gosh, where did you get this?"

"It was easy. The hospital gave me a list of contacts. Besides, since you only have two steps and the incline is modest, I got a portable one. Now you can travel anywhere."

"Yeah, right! I don't plan on doing any traveling but thank you for doing this."

"Well, give it a try. I want to make sure you have the strength to move up the ramp."

Sarah grabs the hand rims and pushes the wheels up the ramp. With extra oomph, she reaches the threshold. Once she's pulled open the screen door, she reaches for the sympathy cards tucked in between the doors. "This doesn't seem like it's been touched for a while. I guess no one's home."

"It's what we expected, right? Apart from that, it's great that you reached the landing on your own. You're a free woman, except there's one more hurdle. You need to unlock the door."

Sarah swivels the chair and inserts the key. The door swings open. "I can't believe I did it."

"I knew you would. But now the real test—inside the house."

Sarah pushes the rims and enters the building. Immediately, she spots a safety rail along the edge of the counter and piles of mail stacked atop it in a heap. She turns and catches Chrissy's mischievous grin.

"You've been busy, haven't you?"

"Let's just say, I know your home well."

Sarah wheels the chair around and smiles at a clean room with fresh flowers on the coffee table. "Chrissy, everything looks beautiful."

"It was nothing, really. Let's go to the bedroom. There's something I want you to see."

Sarah rolls into that back area and notices the bed assist rails. In the adjoining bath, a seat lift and grab bars bring a smile to her face.

"You've thought of everything, Chrissy." She chokes up. "I, I can't thank you enough."

"You'd do the same for me, and you know that to be true. But enough of the touchy-feely stuff. There's more I want to show you. Your jammies are on the bed. Don't bother to remake the bed in the morning and leave a light on—all night. I'll stay with you tonight, to make sure you can handle this. But in the future, I'll come by midday to do the housekeeping— including the wash. Also, here's a medical alert device. Put it on and don't take it off. That's a command. Got it?"

"Really? I'm not an invalid."

"Says the woman in the wheelchair. With this device, you'll get an immediate response if you fall or need help. Otherwise, I won't be able to get a good night's sleep." Chrissy raises her hands, as though Sarah is being impossible.

"I've never had a sister, but for the last five years, you've been both friend and sister. If there's ever anything I can do for you, promise me you'll tell me."

"Have you ever known me to stay quiet?"

"Good point," Sarah says, and they both laugh.

"Okay, enough of that. Follow me. I need to point out a few things in the kitchen." Chrissy opens the refrigerator. "As you can see, the bottom shelves are full. I left the top shelves empty intentionally. You're not to reach that high. Doctor's orders." She moves to the table. "I put the microwave here, so it's easier for you to manage. Don't try to move it. That's an order, too. And you have paper plates and bowls, along with plasticware. After you use them, toss them in the trash. I'll take care of any remaining dishes when I stop by."

"I don't know how I can ever repay your kindness. If only Jack were here . . ."

"But he's not. After the accident, he didn't talk to any of us. I think he blamed himself."

"How could he? I was driving."

"Yeah, but he felt it should have been him in the car and you and the kids at home."

"But . . ."

"It's not rational, so don't fret over it. He's lost in his own messed-up world. About a week ago, he called and stammered out words that made little sense. From what I understood, your doctor explained the severity of your injuries and warned him that you might never wake up. The news shattered him, and grief stole what fragments of a life he had left. That was the last I heard from him."

"I don't know what to say, but I need to know he's safe."

"Same here, but there's not much either of us can do. And, changing the subject, if you're feeling okay, I'll leave for thirty minutes or so to run some errands, but I'll be back. Don't worry."

· · · ◆ ◆ ◆ · · ·

Sarah rolls her chair into the living room. Her eyes move from one item to another and pause at the family photo on the fireplace mantle. *We were a happy family. There was never a quiet moment. Babies chattering or singing, and sometimes crying. Jack crawling on his knees pretending to be a bear or tossing balls in the air.* Her head falls with the weight of the sweet memories while tears drown the frivolity. *Our home has become a tomb.*

Sarah wheels into the bedroom and shudders at the empty stillness. Gone are the arms that once held her, the heartbeat that pounded next to her. *Where are you, Jack? You were my rock, my everything.*

She locates her phone on the side table and calls Jack's office. "Hello, this is Mrs. Jameson. I'm wondering if Jack is available?"

"Jack? He hasn't been here for a couple of weeks. He took a personal leave."

She thanks the man and calls a neighbor.

"Jane, it's Sarah. By chance have you seen Jack?"

"Oh my gosh, Sarah, you're home?"

"My sister-in-law drove me here a few minutes ago."

"Thank God. We've all prayed for you and your family. I can't imagine the sorrow you both must feel. Too much, simply too much."

"Thank you for your prayers and concerns. Jack?"

"I've not noticed him for a week, maybe more. He had a pickup, but he must have returned it to the rental agency. I wish I knew more."

Sarah thanks her friend and considers one more phone call. She punches in the number of their minister.

"Hello, Sarah. I'm relieved you're getting better. The entire congregation has been praying for you."

"Thank you, Pastor Davis. I've felt your intervention and, someday, I'll explain how. But right now, there's something I need to ask."

"Anything, my dear."

"Have you heard from Jack? No one in the family knows where he is."

"Unfortunately, no. The last exchange I had with him was after the funeral. He was inconsolable and didn't want to talk. Not to me. Not to anyone."

CHAPTER 14

FIRST CONTACT

Time blurs when dreams fade. The present, without its past, drifts obscurely before us. We see it but only vaguely. Like a stranger in a foreign land, we wander alone. What was, no longer *is*. But what remains feels like a hologram—unreal and elusive.

Sarah goes through the motions of life. She smiles, even laughs, but in her heart, a terrible loneliness dwells. She lives in between worlds and is unsure about either.

Every morning, Sarah endures physical therapy. She pushes and pulls, stretches and resists. She's determined to walk again, and her determination is rewarded. After many sessions of intensive outpatient exercises, she finally moves unaided through the parallel bars. Sarah holds tightly to the cold metal and takes one unsteady step after another. To her surprise, when she finishes the assignment, her therapist claps.

"You've graduated," he announces.

"What do you mean?"

"You're ready for a walker." He picks up an aluminum-wheeled device, adjusts the legs to her height, and sets it in front of her.

"Really? Are you sure?"

"Trust me, I've worked with patients for years. Just follow my instructions. Slowly, let go of the bars and take hold of the handgrips." He watches as she heeds his instructions. "Good job! Now, take small steps, and lift the device as needed when you move forward."

Sarah hesitates and starts to fall, but the rubber caps on each leg hold the walker in place. A few steps, and she beams. "I'm doing it."

"Of course, you are. My patients always succeed. I make sure of it."

"Does this mean I won't need the wheelchair anymore?"

"It means you're on your way to freedom. Use the chair if you get tired, but otherwise, stick with the walker."

Playfully, Sarah shuffles around the room and marvels at her success. "I worried I might never feel free again. But look at me. I'm walking! Thank you for all your help."

"You've more work ahead of you, but this is a milestone. Go home and find a way to celebrate. My assistant will accompany you downstairs and carry the walker while you ride in the chair. Today's class is dismissed."

Sarah takes the elevator to the first floor and hails a cab. She can barely contain her excitement and thinks, *This is a graduation I'll never forget.* She wipes away a tear as she thanks the assistant for her help.

A few minutes later, the driver pulls up at her home and stops near the entry. The young man rushes out of the taxi to open the door for her. "Do you need assistance?"

"Thank you, sir, I'm fine. But if you could bring the walker to the door, it would help me immensely."

"Of course. I'm here for you."

At her door, Sarah says, "I'd love it if you could pick me up tomorrow morning at seven-thirty."

"I'll be here waiting for you."

Sarah unlocks the door. Smiling at her success, she waves to the driver. Once inside, she surveys the space. Her eyes sadden when she thinks about her life, pre- and post-accident. But then she sees the family photo on the fireplace mantle. A soft smile forms on her lips. Today I found freedom. Now I will make this house a home again.

With the walker, Sarah moves slowly to the couch and sits in front of the coffee table. The simple stand has become her prayer altar. The hospital chaplain had suggested she create such a space and adorn it with items she loves. Sarah followed her advice and set her grandmother's cross in the center of the table. In front of it, she placed her bible. On either side of these sentimental treasures, Sarah positioned photos of her infants and a wedding picture of Jack and her.

She lights the candles at either side of her bible and opens the pages to Mark 11: 24. *Therefore I tell you, whatever you ask in prayer, believe that you have received it, and it will be yours.*

Sarah leans back onto the cushioned couch, closes her eyes, and within minutes, disappears into a blessed Silence.

The ring of Sarah's cell phone jars her back to the present. It's her sister-in-law.

"Chrissy, did you hear from Jack?"

"I got a postcard today. Only a few words on it—*I'm okay. Love you. Jack.*"

"A return address?"

"None, but it's stamped, Burgos."

"Where is that?"

"Spain. I had to Google it. The card has a photograph of a cathedral on it. Nothing else."

"But why there?"

"The only answer I've come up with is the *Camino de Santiago* trail. He and his Marine buddy used to talk about hiking it. That was before he met you."

"Hmm, I've heard people mention it, even refer to it as a pilgrimage."

"I only know the *Camino* is The Way of St. James. Supposedly, after St. James was martyred, his followers transported his remains to Spain and buried him on a hill. Centuries later, the cathedral of Santiago de Compostela was built on top of this burial location. Apparently, miracles have occurred to some who've hiked across the country to that site. But all the pilgrims seem to believe their lives transform."

Sarah exhales slowly. "That makes sense to me. Jack needs alone time to figure things out, and a pilgrimage can do just that."

"He's hardly the praying type."

"We don't need words to pray. Our feet can do it for us."

"I never thought of it that way, but you're right. At least we know he's okay and where he is. Maybe you'll get a card."

"Maybe. But he doesn't know I'm alive. When he left, I was unconscious, and the prognosis wasn't good. I take it he didn't leave an address for mail drops?"

"Nope. None that he's mentioned to me. My brother can be very frustrating. If you hear from him, you'll call me, right?"

"Of course. Thank you for everything."

"You're like a sister to me, Sarah, and always will be. We're in this together. I know it's a bit mushy, but I love you."

Sarah wipes away a tear and admires the smiling faces in the pictures of her precious babies. She takes a deep breath and whispers, "I love you too."

On her phone, Sarah searches for Burgos and finds it's Stage 13 of the French Way on the Camino. She estimates a week or more for mail travel and judges Jack to be between Leon and Astorga—perhaps the small, tranquil town of San Martin Del Camino.

After closing her eyes, Sarah travels through the familiar Silence, across the expanse of time and terrain, over the Gulf of Biscay, to the small Spanish town of San Martin Del Camino. Jack's alive, and she needs to find him.

Through the meditation haze, she finds a well-trodden trail. There, she observes a group of pilgrims with trekking poles. Her spirit draws near and follows. Soon, she keeps pace with one of them.

Bent with the weight of his backpack, this man's steps are strong and unfaltering. Sarah recognizes that stride. She purses her lips and whispers in the wind, "I love you, Jack." He stops, mouth falling open, and turns around. She whispers again, "I love you." And with these words, the man sits on the craggy path and weeps. Sarah's heart melts with tenderness. She's reached him. Now he knows she's alive.

As the wind picks up, Sarah brushes aside a lock of hair that hangs over Jack's eyes. He recognizes the movement. Whenever they'd embrace, she would run her hand through his tousled mop. Her husband whispers, "I love you too."

Sarah draws a deep breath and smiles through her tears. The Divine Silence led her to Jack and dissolved the distance between them. When she opens her eyes, she beams and feels confident that, in another couple of weeks, Jack will come home.

CHAPTER 15

THE SOUL WHISPERER

One week later, Sarah saunters out of her house and down the ramp with the support of her walker. Today, a small backpack hangs across her back. As she reaches the driveway, her cab arrives.

"Ma'am, am I late?"

"No, not at all. I woke up early and got ready faster than usual. That gave me time to make something for you."

"For me?"

"Yes, sir. Just a minute." Sarah pulls a bag from her backpack. "Here you go."

The man peeks inside and his eyes light up when he finds two warm muffins. "Ohhh, you're too nice."

"Naw. You've been extra patient with me, and I'm incredibly grateful."

A few minutes later, the driver pulls in front of the hospital and opens the cab door for her. "You've made my day, ma'am. I don't get many riders who are kind like you. Thank you."

"Well, if you don't, you should. You're the best." Sarah waves good-bye and progresses into the hospital and up to the physical therapy floor. She enters the familiar complex and finds her therapist busy with a set of weights.

"Mornin', Sarah. I'll be with you in a minute. I'm adjusting these weights for the next patient. If you don't have any questions, go ahead and begin your routine. I'll watch you from here."

Sarah starts on the parallel bars. She glances back at her therapist and notices his watchful gaze.

"You're doing great, Sarah. Okay, make another lap." He steps next to the bars and asks how she feels.

"Like I could walk a mile." She says with a mischievous smile.

"I thought as much. I want you to try moving without touching the bars. If you feel unsteady, reach for them."

Initially, Sarah hesitates but then drops her arms and moves unassisted between the bars.

The therapist observes Sarah's increased mobility and smiles with pride. "You're ready for the next level. Your gait is steady and strong. I'd like you to try a quad cane."

He reaches to hand her one, and at the same time, Dr. Roberts strides into the complex. "So, how's our patient?"

"She's doing great. Already progressed to a quad cane."

"Good. I want to put her to work." He grins at Sarah. "I've followed your progress and think you can handle it. Are you ready to meet with a patient?"

"In the way you described before? Accompanying the person?"

"Exactly. We have a middle-aged man, who's unresponsive. His vitals are weak, but I think if you spoke with him, he might pull out."

"That's quite an assumption, Doctor." Sarah frowns at the tiled floor and considers her answer. "I'll speak with him, but I don't want you to be disappointed if he doesn't pull through. We don't control the time or day."

"I understand that, and I won't feel disappointed one way or the other, but I'm interested in what you perceive once you're with him. When's this session over?" He glances at the therapist.

"She's finished for the day."

"Okay then, shall we go together, Sarah?"

··◆◆◆··

On crisp white sheets, Benjamin O'Malley lies comatose. With the lights dimmed in his private room, an eerie hush permeates. Only the bleeps from the heart monitor offer signs of life.

Distant hallway voices rise and fall through the ajar door. Medical staff talk of procedures and supplies, unaware the dying man hears them.

Benjamin's spirit lifts from the bed and hovers above his lifeless form. Perplexed, he examines the face he wore for fifty-two years. *How strange to see what I thought was me. I imagined myself more handsome and robust than this.*

A rushing sound captures his attention, and he turns to observe a tunnel drawing near. A strong magnetic field pulls him forward, but unsure of what lies ahead, he resists and yells out in soundlessness. *More time. I need more time!*

At the warning beep of his heart monitor, two nurses rush into the cubicle and to the side of the bed.

"Do we resuscitate? What's in his healthcare directive?"

Laila shakes her head. "He doesn't have one."

"Any loved ones nearby?"

"From what I heard, the guy didn't have many, or any, friends."

"Makes you wonder, doesn't it? A wasted life?"

The man struggles to speak, but no one can hear him. *My life wasn't wasted, and it's not over. I'm here, and there's more I need to do. I've got meetings about the upcoming merger. I don't have time for this.*

Laila grimaces as she monitors the vitals, oblivious to Benjamin's hovering spirit. "The dude is supposedly wealthy. But look at him. What does he really have?"

"Pitiful, isn't it?" Pam darts a glance at her friend. "Rich but destitute. There's not even a phone number to call. Surely there's someone somewhere who loved him."

"This isn't the first patient I've seen like this. There was a time when I envied the rich. They seem to have it easy. You know what I mean, don't you?"

"Yeah. They're not pulling night shifts, that's for sure."

"Well, neither are we, but we're not wearing white gloves either." Laila pulls out her phone. "I'll buzz Dr. Roberts. The monitor's stopped bleeping."

From his comatose state, Benjamin calls out to the nurses. *No, no, no. I'm here. I need more time. Don't you understand?*

They don't understand because they cannot hear him.

Dr. Roberts rushes in with Sarah close behind. He checks the monitor for a rhythm. "There's a sporadic faint bleep. We should wait. It won't be long now. I'll be down the hall, so call if there's a development. By the way, this is Sarah. I've asked her to sit with this man."

The nurses watch the doctor leave, and then Pam addresses Sarah, "What's going on?"

"Dr. Roberts asked me to visit with Mr. O'Malley to offer support. I'll try not to interfere with your work."

Pam's forehead furrows, "Have we met? You seem familiar."

"It's been a while, but yes. I worked in Surgical Intensive Care until my accident. Sarah Jameson."

"Yes, yes. A month ago?"

"Correct. Dr. Roberts invited me back to the hospital to help with comatose patients. Sometimes a chaplain isn't available, especially in the Emergency Room and Intensive Care Units, and he convinced me that I could help comfort dying patients."

Laila says, "I'm glad you've come. This man appears to have no relatives or friends. We were wondering about saying a prayer."

"Very thoughtful of you. Your name?"

"Laila. Laila Brown. My friend, here, is Pam Sutherland."

"Wonderful to meet you both. Excuse me, but I'd better attend to Mr. O'Malley. Could you pull over a chair for me? It's difficult to do with the cane."

Laila moves a chair next to the bed and watches.

Leaning against the bed, Sarah rests her hand on the patient.

"Hello, Mr. O'Malley, my name is Sarah, and together we'll take a journey." In a slow monotone manner, she continues, "I know this is scary, but you're not alone. Listen to my voice. I'll help you step by step."

But I can't die now. I've too much to do. Can you hear me?

Laila and Pam take notice as Sarah rubs the man's hand while she whispers about the gift death brings. "Every love you've ever known awaits you. Every tender exchange is yours to experience again. Settle into your heart . . ."

A soft glow surrounds Sarah as she speaks, and when the monitor sounds, she turns to the nurses. "It's best you don't remove the life support. But could you turn off the alarm? I need a few more minutes."

"I'll do that, but why? What's the use?"

"He's unsettled. I believe he may take a breath soon."

Pam shuts off the buzzer and turns to Laila, who lifts her shoulders in a *what-can-it-hurt* motion.

Sarah continues to whisper to the patient and touches the side of his face gently. Almost five minutes later, the heart monitor bleeps and continues. He lives.

When Sarah shifts away from the bed, she notices her wide-eyed colleagues and shrugs. "We think we control life, but we don't. It's a gift, and every moment is precious. Few people get a second chance, but this gentleman has."

"Why him and not others?"

"It would take me a while to explain, but this man fought death as he fought life. He's decided to return to learn how to love life. It won't be easy for him because of his injuries. Let me know what happens, okay."

With those few words, Sarah shuffles toward the door.

"Someday will you tell us what you said to him?"

Sarah nods. "It's nothing mysterious. I simply tried to meet him on the other side of life and then shared what I saw, and what I felt. The final steps are his alone." Sarah offers a quick wave and leaves the room as Dr. Roberts enters.

"How are you holding up?"

"I'm doing well."

"They need help in the ER. Would you mind?"

"I'll go, but will they understand why I'm there?"

"I'm calling them now."

Sarah walks into the elevator while Dr. Roberts makes the call.

·· ◆ ◆ ··

The doctor returns to Mr. O'Malley's room and observes the quizzical expressions of the nurses. He nods and says, "I call her the Soul Whisperer."

"We ... I ..."

"No worries. She's not ready to assume full nursing responsibilities, so I asked her to sit with dying patients to calm their fears." He gazes at the monitor and sees a heartbeat. Dr. Roberts smiles. "Mr. O'Malley seems to have taken a turn for the better. I'll check his other vitals."

"Doctor, he died about five minutes ago, but Sarah asked us to keep life support active while she talked to him. And—"

Dr. Roberts says, "And his heart began beating."

"Yes, Doctor."

"I suspected as much. I've seen it before. Not that I understand it, but I've seen it. Sometimes a patient defies medical determinants."

Pam moves nearer to the body. "I asked Sarah what she said to Mr. O'Malley, and she said she shared what she felt and saw. Does that make sense to you?"

The doctor takes a deep breath, "Sense? I'm not sure, but if I were in a similar state, I'd want her by my side."

"Me too."

"Are you aware of her near-death experience? Her accident?"

"No, but I assumed something tragic because of her obvious condition."

"A drunk hit her broadside. She lost her two kids, a three-year-old son, and a baby daughter. And, of course, she suffered temporary loss of function."

Pam gasps and covers her mouth with her hand.

"No one thought she'd pull through."

"Her husband?"

"Don't know. He sat bedside for the first couple of weeks. But I don't believe he's been around recently."

"She doesn't talk about it?"

"Not to me. Our friendship is a professional one, and I haven't ventured into her personal life."

"I'm surprised she's working."

"As I mentioned, it's a special assignment. She's a well-trained volunteer."

CHAPTER 16

EMERGENCY ROOM

Alarms sound at the emergency entrance at County Central Hospital, and medical teams rush to assist the incoming patients from separate ambulances. The paramedics push two gurneys through the entry doors and shout, "Code Blue."

The first patient is a young woman in traumatic distress. Attacked and severely beaten at an ATM, she suffers compound fractures and internal injuries.

The girl's mother scrambles to keep up with the medics. "I'm here, darling."

The victim gurgles slow breaths and reaches for her mother.

A nurse insists, "You must move out of the way, ma'am."

"I won't leave my daughter. Not now. Not ever."

"Then stand back. Your daughter needs immediate attention."

The mother's lips quiver, but she moves backward, out of the way, and watches as the doctor works, frantically, to try to save her child. The woman recognizes the desperation on his face and anticipates what lies ahead. She calls out, "I'm here, dear. Don't be afraid. You're not alone. You will be with Papa soon, and I will join you later."

Upon hearing the final rattle of breath and the time of death recorded, the mother breaks down in tears. A nurse goes to her side, gently rubs her back, and invites her to say her goodbyes to her child.

The mother approaches the bed and bends to kiss her daughter's hand. Barely recognizable because of the trauma, the once beautiful young woman now lies lifeless. The desolate woman strokes the girl's curly brown hair and falls into a nearby chair. The nurse explains the next steps, but the mother doesn't hear the words. She's lost in the forsaken moment where time stands still.

Sarah hurries into the room and signals to the nurse. "I'm Sarah Jameson."

"We've been expecting you."

Sarah walks over to the mother, and a gentle breeze swirls around the gathering. The mother lifts her eyes heavenward and then to Sarah.

"She's gone, isn't she?"

Sarah nods and wraps her arm around the woman's shoulder. "Yes. She's at peace."

"My sweet child is Home. Someday, we'll be a family again. At least I can rest, knowing she's preparing the way."

An attending nurse restrains her tears, and the doctor explains that he'll come back shortly.

"Mrs. Sampson—" Sarah says, "—maybe you'd like to take a chair in the hallway for a few minutes. The team has work to do, and I'd like to talk with you."

The mother looks up at Sarah and at her daughter. "She's part of me. I should be with her."

"Absolutely, but let's step out for a few minutes so the nurses can do their work and we can chat."

The grieving mother follows Sarah into the hall, and the nurses remove the central lines, the heart monitor, and the sensors.

Sarah reaches for the grief-stricken mother. "Death seems so final, doesn't it?"

"Yes, yes, of course."

"I always thought it as such, until I died."

The mother focuses on Sarah and takes her hand. "You? Ah, you . . ."

"It's true. Officially, I died during surgery, but obviously, I recovered. What I want you to know is that it was a blissful experience. I saw my babies, who perished in the same accident as me. They were radiant and so happy. I still hear their laughter and, sometimes, I feel them near."

"Was there fear? Pain?"

"Neither. You felt the soft breeze around your daughter, didn't you?"

"Uh-huh."

"And you knew."

"Yes. I knew she was gone."

"Home."

The mother wipes away a tear. "Home."

Down the corridor, multiple loud voices sound out. Armed officers shackle a man to his bed, while the man shouts profanities.

"I believe that's the man who killed my daughter. I need to talk with the police."

"I'll go with you."

Mrs. Sampson's lips tighten when she stands and trudges to the uniformed men. Blood stains their arms. She asks, "Are you the officers who tried to help my daughter?"

They turn to the distraught woman. Sarah stands next to her and empathizes with her grief-rimmed eyes.

"My daughter. You tried to help her?"

"Yes, we responded. We did what we could. How is she?"

"She's no longer with us."

The first officer closes his hands in hard fists and, through tight lips, spits out, "It's not right. It's not right." He points to the bay. "The perp will live, but only behind bars, if I have anything to say."

The second officer grimaces his agreement.

The prisoner screams out in pain. "I have my rights. Take off these cuffs, you animals." The man struggles against the metal restraints and kicks at everyone.

Behind the curtain, the attending nurse darts a glance at the doctor and gets his nod. With the officers' help and hospital staff's assistance, she ensures both legs are secured to the gurney. Then she gives the criminal the shot ordered by the doctor. "This will help with your pain."

"You bitch! Why should I, ah, I . . ."

Within seconds, the man collapses onto the bed, and the ER team begins the task of cleaning and preparing the unidentified man. The doctor examines his shoulder wound. "Clean shot. Missed arteries. Bullet passed through."

The nurses stand and wait for the doctor's signal.

The doctor side-glances the nurses. "I'll stitch him up. Let's get him prepped." Once finished, and taking a deep breath, he leaves the team to talk with the officers, Mrs. Sampson, and Sarah.

The lead officer scowls. "Can he be released today?"

"He can, but he'll need daily medical attention until the wound heals."

"Not a problem. We'll take care of it." He motions with his eyes to the mother of the victim, and the doctor understands.

"Ma'am, are you the mother of the young woman?"

"Yes, Doctor. I want to ask him why. Why did he kill my beautiful daughter?"

"He's sedated right now, ma'am, but I doubt he'll ever answer that question for you. Sometimes only faith can help us understand." He touches her hand, and with fallen shoulders, he returns to the ER bay.

"I believe the nurses are finished with the final procedures," Sarah says. "Would you like to be with your daughter? You've seventeen wonderful years to say goodbye to, even though she's near."

"Please, I'd be so grateful."

5000 MILES AWAY

At the close of another day of physical therapy and spiritual support to dying patients, Sarah wanders outside and hails a cab. She thought about strolling home by herself but decided the two miles might be difficult for her to manage. She's had a long day. *Maybe tomorrow.*

Sarah gets in the cab and scoots across the cracked leather seat. As the driver pulls away, she catches a whiff of greasy cuisine. She forces a smile as waves of carsickness hit with each bounce and jerk of the old Chevrolet. When the car comes to a stop in her driveway, she gulps down her discomfort and pays the man the fare.

Slowly, she walks to the neighborhood's clustered mailboxes and feels faint. She tightens her grip on the quad cane and pauses for a few minutes. *Maybe I got out of the car too quickly. Perhaps it's that awful smell.* Sarah takes a deep breath and leans on the mailbox until the lightheadedness lifts. With the mail in hand, she heads up the ramp to the front door.

Each day Sarah returns home with one hope—to find Jack with open arms, ready for an embrace. When she opens the door, her knees weaken, and her shoulders sag. The house is dark, and she faces another evening alone.

After releasing a hard sigh, Sarah flips on the lights and collapses onto the couch. She examines the mail gathered on her lap and sifts through the envelopes—nothing from her husband, not even a postcard. The last time Sarah saw Jack was right before the accident, months prior. After she'd completed a split shift at the hospital, she sauntered home and fell into his open arms. Always, the warmth of his embrace soothed the strains of the day. Then she kissed the babies.

Unwanted memories from that fatal day flood Sarah, and none of them seem real. She recalls singing as she drove to the grocery store and the light turning green. Then all goes black. Another wave of nausea fills the emptiness, and Sarah shudders. With a deep breath, she gets up and grabs a bottle of water from the refrigerator.

Sarah takes slow sips and reminds herself of the choice she made—to return for Jack's sake. She shuffles over to the couch and gazes at her makeshift prayer altar. *Maybe I can reach him again.* She lights the two candles, closes her eyes, and pushes back into the cushions.

· · · ◆ ◆ ◆ · · ·

More than 5,000 miles away, Jack startles awake, confused as to his location. Panting, he looks, furtively, across the dimly lit space and realizes he's in a hostel. Cot after cot holds a pilgrim, and the room echoes with random coughs and snores. He remembers choosing his cot, next to his buddy Mateo and slows his breath. *Ponferrada—we arrived late afternoon yesterday and stood under a medieval clock tower. We had sausages and wine near the Castle of the Templars.*

Rain pelts the hostel roof, and an electrical strike hits nearby. Jack ducks under his sleeping bag. He's back in the war. *Mortars pound the earth, and shells from M16s shish by him.* He tells himself it's not real, and yet he shakes. Even with his eyes squinted shut, he sees the Afghani children again—big-eyed and covered in dirt. And they're not alone. His own two little ones stand next to them.

"No, no, no!" he cries to no one. "You shouldn't have died. If only I had reached you sooner. If only . . ."

Matt shakes him. "Jack, JACK! You're having a nightmare. Wake up."

Blanched with fear, Jack peers up at his friend.

"You're not in Kamdesh. The Afghanistan war is over. Get that in your thick head."

"I try. I really try. But since the accident, ah, I keep seeing two Afghani kids—and mine. They're all dead, and they just stare at me. I know it's not real, but they stand there as real as you sit by me."

"You think it's your fault they're dead, don't you?"

"Well . . . if I'd gotten there a few minutes earlier."

"Really? Think about what you're saying. Who killed those Afghani kids?"

"The Taliban."

"And your *if only*, how does that play out in your brain? Be concrete. I want to hear it."

"If, ah, if the Captain had sent us in earlier—"

"So, it's the Captain's fault."

"I didn't say that."

"Yeah, you did. The lazy butt should have sent you in earlier."

"I didn't say that."

"Well, tell me again. If only . . ."

Jack shoos a fly that buzzes around his head and focuses on the tile floor. He fumbles for words, "I, I don't know. I just wish I could have done something to help those kids."

"And you didn't?"

"I tried. You were there. You know. We were in a hailstorm of bullets."

"You're right about that. So why were we there?"

"To help the people."

"Exactly. We weren't there for target practice or a card game. We risked our lives to save the Afghanis. Some of us didn't make it back, like Jimmy."

"I get your point."

"What about your kids?"

Jack scratches the back of his neck and grimaces. "There was nothing I could do."

"All right! We've got a long hike ahead of us, and I'm starving. So, let's finish this up. Remember what Jesus said about forgiveness? Seventy times seven. When you start blaming yourself again, stop and say, 'I forgive you, Jack.' Got it?"

"Whatever."

"Hell no. I don't want to go over this again. What are you going to say to yourself, Marine?"

Jack draws back and glowers at his persistent friend. With his lips puckered, he retorts, "I forgive you, Jack."

Mateo narrows his dark brown eyes and studies his friend. "Let's get dressed and find some breakfast. We need to hit the trail. By the way, how are your blisters?"

"Not great. I'll survive."

His buddy tosses him a package. "Hikers Wool. Ever used it?"

"Nah."

"It's a necessity. Wherever it's tender, put a wad. Then put on your socks. It'll stay in place."

"Thanks. Sorry to be a pain. I packed quickly, and I'm not as prepared as I should be."

"For God's sake, stop the garbage talk. We're here, we're hungry, and we have miles ahead of us. It's that simple."

Jack looks over at his buddy and tries, unsuccessfully, to restrain a smirk. "Oohrah!"

Matt draws a breath and shoves his friend. "Let's get our rain gear on and find some food. We'll come back for the rest after we eat."

A few minutes later, they sit across from each other in a small cafe. Drizzle slides down the windows and obscures the view.

"Maybe we should do something indoors today. We've got the time."

Jack takes a long sip of his coffee. "You've something in mind?"

"Yeah. Centuries ago, the Knights Templars had their headquarters here. I'd like to go tour the castle. A lot of history there."

"I'm all in. I don't know much about the Templars, except that they were extraordinary soldiers. You might need to translate for me."

"Been doing that all along, buddy."

CHAPTER 18

BETWEEN WORLDS

Sunlight pours through the walls of windows that enclose the physical therapy complex. The bright light prompts Sarah to say, "With the monsoon rains, I almost forgot what a sunny day looks like."

The therapist grins. "Soon you'll be romping around in that sunlight. With your progress . . . umm . . . maybe another week of PT."

"You're serious?"

"I don't joke about recovery times. Today, I'll check your range of motion as you go through the exercises. Then I'll decide for sure. And if I'm right, you'll have to find your sunshine elsewhere."

Sarah chuckles. "I think you're overly optimistic about the time frame, but I'm ready for sunshine anytime and anywhere."

The therapist points to the bars. "Let's get going." As Sarah goes through the exercise steps, he evaluates her progress. At the end of the procedures, he announces, "You won't need me in another couple of days.

"No way."

"Yes, way. If you feel safer using a cane, then do so, but it's your call entirely. Today, I'm shifting your training to repetitive, weight-bearing tasks. These movements will help you rebuild muscle strength. And you can do them at home."

He directs her to the other side of the room.

While they work, two ambulances blare as they pull into the emergency entrance of the hospital, which sits below the therapy room. Sarah excuses herself, hurries to the window, and squints down at the entrance, she observes a medical team donning gowns and gloves as they hurry to the patients.

"I may need to leave early today. If so, would that be okay?"

"You've gone through the exercises, and you can do more at home. So, yes, it's fine. Here's a sheet with diagrams for each of the movements. Try to incorporate the routines in your daily life."

Sarah's cell buzzes a text alert from an ER nurse. *If you're nearby, we've two unresponsive teenagers.*

She texts back. *I'll be there in a few.*

Sarah turns to the physical therapist and asks, "Tomorrow?"

"Tomorrow it is."

"Thank you. I'll be here promptly at seven." Sarah hurries out of the complex and exits the elevator at the same time as the new patients are rushed inside separate ER bays.

A paramedic shouts as he darts into a bay, "Found in an ally, unresponsive. Drug overdose. Administered Naloxone. No reaction. Skin ulcerated, most likely injection sites along with possible scabies. No identification."

A second paramedic echoes the first. "Same here. Unresponsive. No reaction to Naloxone. Scars and sores all over the arms and legs. No identification."

Sarah watches as the attending ER physician adds a full mask to his body cover, and then checks the patients. "This one has no pulse. Did you try to resuscitate?"

"Yes, Doctor. I thought I felt a beat."

"There's none now. I'll check the other." The doctor puts his fingers on the groove next to the patient's windpipe and holds it against the carotid artery. "She's got a faint pulse. Hook her up and call housekeeping to bag these clothes and get them out of here."

Downcast, the two emergency responders walk past Sarah, their frustration evident in their every move.

"Somedays it feels like it's no use," the first says to the other.

"Maybe our few minutes of care is more than they've experienced for months or years."

"True. That's one way to understand it, but how sad is that?"

They shake their heads, climb into their ambulances, and drive away.

Sarah refocuses on the ER bays and watches the doctor. Red-faced, he betrays his anger as he calls the time of death for the second patient. She listens to his rant. "Every week, we get a kid who's overdosed on Tranq, the Frankenstein opioids. This can't continue. Something must be done. Any person who supports open borders should spend a week in this ER. We're the last resort, and usually, they're dead when they arrive."

A nurse says, "Couldn't agree more, Doctor. I've contacted Social Services to add these two patients to their list of unidentified bodies. Maybe they'll be able to track down a relative."

Sarah bites her lower lip as her eyes drift back to the doctor. She understands his frustration. He, and the whole team, work hard to help critically injured or ill patients.

The doctor says, "You know as well as I, if they can't find a relative these two will end up cremated, like most of the other unnamed deceased."

Sarah listens to the nurse's explanation about why they must make the effort and remembers saying the same thing, almost word for word.

But the doctor won't have it. "Of course, but if that *someone* cared, don't you think he or she would have gotten the patient some help before now?"

Sarah's been in their positions many times. Too many times. The attending nurse offers a weak response, "Maybe they tried." But her words aren't enough.

The doctor fumes. "This one can't be more than fifteen. The other may be eighteen. Who are the parents?" With those questions, he storms out of the room and goes to a decontamination area to pull off his protective gown.

The nurse studies the two patients and shakes her head, saying to her colleague, "He's right. It's a hopeless task."

"Yeah. It's hard to work in the ER. It demands detachment. Even if we saved these two, then what? They'd be back—unless they're sent directly to the morgue."

"You have kids?"

"Three."

"I've two. Got them in a private school, but that's no guarantee they're protected."

··✦✦✦··

Above the confusion, the fifteen-year-old gawks at her disfigured body. *No one understands. I couldn't stop. I tried, but I needed it to survive, or at least I thought I did. The vomiting, the pain, I had no choice. I'm not a bad person. I'm not. I want my mom and dad. Where are they?*

The nurse shakes her head, peers out to the hallway, and spots Sarah. "Thank goodness you're here. Come on in. We need help, and Dr. Roberts said you can assist."

Sarah stands beside the youngest victim. "How long since she passed?"

"Maybe five minutes. Here's a gown. I'll get you some gloves. She's covered in sores."

Sarah puts on the gloves and takes the young woman's hand. She whispers to the girl, who says, *"Tell them. Please. Tell them I'm here. I don't understand what's happening. Why won't people fix me?"*

Sarah continues to whisper and lets her head fall. Solemnly, she moves to the other bed and begins the same ritual. While she stares at the boy, she asks, "When did he pass?"

"I'm not sure but ten minutes is a fair guess. We did what we could, but he had no pulse when he arrived."

Sarah touches the boy's hand. "He's left already. I can't help him now."

Pam approaches Sarah. "I don't know what you say or why, but maybe we could have lunch someday and chat?"

"I look forward to that."

When Sarah leaves the ER, Dr. Roberts walks down the hallway, headed her way. She smiles and offers a wave.

"How are you doing, Sarah? I see you're standing without your cane."

"You noticed. I've got great news. I graduated today, and I've progressed to repetitive exercises."

With a gleam in his eyes, Roberts says, "You must have had the help of a great surgeon."

"The best. And I have a question for that amazing doctor."

"Let me hear it."

"I've had flares of nausea and some dizziness. Do you think that's residual from the anesthesia?"

"It's a possibility and being in a coma also can have a lingering impact. I'll order a full blood workup, just to make sure all's well. I'll order a fasting draw, so no food before the blood test. Will tomorrow morning work?"

"Absolutely. I'll be at the lab first thing."

"Let's meet in a week. I'll go over the blood results and do a post-op exam. If necessary, I'll order further tests, but I'm optimistic your queasiness is the result of the lengthy coma."

CHAPTER 19

SURROUNDED BY LOVE

On this early morning, Sarah awakens to the warbles of two gold-finches outside her bedroom window. She imagines them to be her children chirping *hello* and beams with joy. "I know you're here, dear ones. Thank you for the visit." She sits up and smooths Jack's side of the bed. "I need your help to find Daddy. Can you do that for me?"

Sarah looks around the room and her eyes rest on a photo taken at the Grand Canyon. Jack and she had hiked halfway down the Canyon trailhead and, exhausted, had struggled back up the rocky path. A tourist took the photo when they reached the surface. Sarah laughs when she recalls the playfulness of that journey and the challenge. "We've more adventures ahead of us, Jack. Don't give up."

Sarah climbs out of bed and checks the clock—5:30 a.m. With a stretch toward the ceiling, she takes a deep breath and decides that today she will walk to the hospital. *I've got plenty of time. I can do this.*

Forty-five minutes later, she begins her trek and her new life.

As she ambles past her neighbor's home, she pauses at the brilliance of the rose hedge lining the side of the yard. Sunlight glimmers from the morning dew, and the scarlet blossoms vibrate with life. A mini rainbow refracts off the irrigation spray and adds to the grandeur. *Why haven't I noticed this before?* A stranger strides past her, carrying a wrapped newspaper in one hand and a cell phone in the other. "I'm on my way," the man says, and at that moment, Sarah realizes why she hasn't seen what she sees today. She's always been too preoccupied.

Sarah arrives at the hospital lab a couple of minutes after 7:00 a.m.

"Come on in, Ms. Sarah. You're my first patient today. From your expression, I think you must have some happy news to share."

"Kinda. I walked from home to the hospital this morning, two miles, and I did it without help. A couple of months ago, I couldn't stand."

"I remember your situation. It's good to have you on the floors again."

"I'm so glad to be back. I haven't assumed nursing duties yet, but I try to help patients who lie in between life and death."

"I heard about how you talk with the dying. Your work blesses people, Ms. Sarah. It's God's work."

"That's kind of you to say. I certainly hope I'm helping in some small way."

The phlebotomist ties the tourniquet and swabs the vein with alcohol. "I mean it. It's God's work. You help patients at the most critical point of their life."

"I like to think so."

The phlebotomist reviews the order. "This will take a few minutes. Dr. Roberts covered the bases with this request, and I must fill several tubes." As she draws blood, a yellow lightbulb on the wall flashes. "It appears we have incoming air transport. I get notified of accidents in case they need blood drawn."

···◆◆◆◆◆···

An air ambulance lands on the hospital helipad, carrying an unconscious thirty-four-year-old male. The medical crew steps out and shouts over the noise of the rotor blades to the hospital team, who rushes to unload the patient.

"Jeep and motorcycle accident on the Cooper Creek Trail. This guy took the brunt of it. The head-on collision threw his bike in the air. We found him on a boulder, his leg dangling and bleeding badly. His helmet got knocked off, and he's been unconscious this whole time."

A doctor and two nurses move the man onto their gurney. The doctor shouts, "Take him to surgery." Then he turns to the medics, "The driver of the jeep?"

"He was able to walk away."

"Thanks for your help." The doctor hurries after his team.

·· ◆ ◆ ◆ ◆ ··

On the first floor of the hospital, a worried father runs through the entrance in search of his son. Once the staff understands the man's needs, they direct him to the waiting area by the Emergency Room.

While pacing the hallway, he stops one of the nurses. "Please help me. I'm looking for my son. An air ambulance took him here, but I can't find him. Do you know where he is?"

The nurse mentions a few possibilities and makes a call to the surgery unit. She listens and nods, understanding. She turns to the anxious man and says softly, "Sir, your son is in surgery. He's on the fifth floor, and there's a waiting room nearby. It's best you go there."

The man dashes into the elevator, and when it stops on the fifth floor, he steps out and observes medical personnel darting to and fro.

"Step back," a nurse yells at the man.

"My son. Danny Pella. How is he? Where is he?"

"Sir, go to the waiting room."

Mr. Pella's eyes widen as he grows more and more alarmed. He swallows hard, choking out a cough. His heart pounds in his ears, and he loses balance. He grabs the wall sidebar and inches toward the designated room.

Another doctor gets off the elevator and rushes through the surgery doors. This time, Mr. Pella remains silent. He watches. He listens. And he moves inside the waiting room. With his head in his hands, he weeps and prays for his son.

Lost in time—present and past—the man sits alone. Only three years prior, he buried his wife of forty years. He thought he'd never survive her passing, but he did. Now he wonders if he can face the real possibility that his son will join her.

A surgeon's voice draws him out of his dark thoughts. "Mr. Pella?"

"Yes, Doctor."

"I did the best I could. We now wait. Your son sustained critical injuries, and though I have hope he'll survive, I'm realistic. You need to prepare yourself for the worst. Other family members?"

The sorrowful man shakes his head. "My wife passed away several years ago. Danny's only sibling lives hours from here. I'll call her when I know more."

"How old's your son?"

"Thirty-four." He looks away and back to the doctor. "Danny's a bit of a daredevil."

"From what the first responders explained, this accident had nothing to do with your son. It was a freak collision."

The father lifts his head and wipes his watery eyes. "He's a good boy. Likes to help others."

"Well, hopefully soon, he'll be back in the mix of things."

Haltingly, the man says, "I hope so. He's my only son."

A nurse rushes out, "The heart monitor alarm—" She stops short when she recognizes the father. The surgeon hurries after her, back into the room. The father eases up from his chair and waits with his mouth agape.

·· ◆ ◆ ··

Danny's spirit rises above the bed, and he observes with curiosity. *The doctor and nurses look so worried, but I'm fine. Haven't felt better. Why's Dad crying? There's no need. I feel great, Dad.*

The physician works to revive the young man. "Call for Sarah, the one Dr. Roberts works with," he says to the nurse. "Now!"

Minutes later, Sarah enters the recovery room and stands next to the surgeon.

"He's slipping. Thought you might speak with him. Name's Danny. Mother's passed. Father stands in the hall. Tragic situation." The surgeon continues to work furiously, trying to save the young man.

Sarah draws closer to the patient. She takes his hand and brings her head next to his. In a low voice, she says, "Hi, Danny. I'm a friend. I've been where you are, and I know you'll soon make a choice—whether to join your mother or remain here with your father. I want to talk with you about that choice."

While Sarah whispers, the doctor starts resuscitation procedures while a nurse shouts the readings. They attach the defibrillator and use electric shocks to restore a normal heart rhythm, but there's no response.

Danny continues to float above the frantic activity. *Why is everyone so upset? I'm okay. Really, I am. Nice lady, you talk about choices, but I'm here. Can't you see me?*

Sarah grips the young man's hand firmly. "I know you're nearby, Danny. I remember when I died and how I gazed at my body. It's strange to observe oneself as lifeless on a hospital bed. I could hear everything. I tried to tell people. But no one could hear me or see me—the *alive* me. Even though I can't see you or hear you, I know you're listening. Soon, you'll be leaving. Has the tunnel appeared yet?"

The physician shocks Danny again, trying to get a heartbeat. Again. Then again. Finally, he shakes his head, and unable to mask his inner torment, he glances up at the clock and, stoically, calls out the time of death.

But I'm not dead. Why can't people hear me? A bright light approaches and Danny follows.

The doctor regains composure and leaves the room to talk with the father. "Sir, I'm sorry to inform you that your son has passed away. We did all we could, but the injuries were too severe."

The elderly gentleman breaks down. "No! He can't leave. He hasn't had a full life yet. It can't be time."

The doctor directs his attention to Sarah and motions for her to come.

Sarah goes to Mr. Pella and stands by his side. As the man sobs in his anguish, she rubs his back gently. "Would you like to sit with your son? I'll stay with you. Together, we'll say goodbye." The bereaved father nods and follows Sarah to his son's bedside. As soon as he nears his son's lifeless body, he sobs.

"I had hopes," the father laments, "hopes he'd marry and have kids. I dreamt of us being a family again. But he's gone, and so is hope."

Sarah locates a chair for the father and guides him to sit. Finding another one, she scoots next to him.

The grief-stricken man holds his son's limp hand and, through his tears, he tells Sarah about his son. "He was a good kid. Everyone loved him. He'd help a stranger, a friend, anyone he could." He faces Sarah with his red-swollen eyes. "Why would God take him? Why not me? My life is finished. His life was just beginning. Why him? I don't understand."

"I wish I could answer those questions—for you and me. But I don't know. My two precious children died in a car accident. My son was three years old, and my daughter was only eight months. My one comfort is that I was in the same accident and died during surgery. While I was dead, I saw my children. They were ecstatic, running in a field of beautiful flowers. And seeing them as I did—playing joyfully—gives me great comfort. I miss them terribly, but I feel certain they're happy. They're alive in heaven."

"Your, your babies died?"

"Yes, just a couple of months ago."

"I, I'm so sorry."

"As I'm sorry for you, Mr. Pella. There's no worse pain than that of a parent who's lost a child. But realizing a loved one is happy, *very happy,* in heaven, can soften that pain. Your son is at peace now, truly, and he is surrounded by Love."

CHAPTER 20

THE LETTER

Unassisted, Sarah ambles from her home to her physical therapy appointment. Drawing in a breath, she releases her arms toward the heavens. "Thank you, thank you," she shouts as she celebrates her newly earned mobility.

Her neighbor, Jane, notices her joy and drops her gardening spade to wave hello. "Warms my heart to see you so happy, Sarah."

"I thought this day would never come. I can walk freely, and I'm over-the-top excited."

"Yay for you! If you don't mind me asking, have you heard from Jack?"

"I only wish. I believe he's with his Marine buddy—maybe trekking in the wilds. But thank you for asking and for keeping your eyes open for him."

"We're all here for you. If there's ever anything we can do, let us know and consider it done."

Sarah's phone pings with a text. She says her goodbyes and checks the message as she walks away. It's from Dr. Roberts. *Initial blood results are excellent. I'll have a full report next week.*

A big smile stretches across Sarah's face. She clasps her hands to her chest, takes a deep breath, and mutters, "Everything is going to be okay."

Upon entering the lobby of the hospital, Sarah greets the staff enthusiastically and heads to the elevator. She pushes the button on the control panel, but before the doors close, her phone flashes again. It's a text message from the Emergency Room nurse, Laila. *We've got an unresponsive child. Could you help?*

Swiftly, she steps out of the elevator and replies. *I'm down the hall. On my way.* She sends a quick message to the physical therapist and explains an emergency has come up. As she nears the ER, Laila rushes to greet her.

"The child's stopped breathing. Please, hurry. Her name is Trisha."

Laila leads Sarah to the third bay, past the hysterical mother and pacing father, and to the child's side. She leans over the little girl and speaks softly in her ear.

"Trisha, darling, I'm a friend, and I want to chat with you."

Can you tell my mom and dad that I'm okay? Really, I am. I feel great. I don't know why they are crying.

"I know you can hear me, and I know you're trying to respond, but we can't hear you. Only you can hear what everyone says."

You're right. I hear you, lady, but I don't understand what's going on. Do you?

"Soon a big tunnel will manifest. It leads to a magical place. Sometimes we have a choice between that special life or our families. Maybe you have a choice, and if so, you can decide if you want to stay there or come back home with your mommy and daddy, who love you very much."

Oh, there's a beautiful garden with huge butterflies. There are lots of children. I want to play too.

"Though I can't hear you, I know you're listening to me. I once went down the tunnel. It was so beautiful on the other side, and I didn't want to come back. But my family needed me, so I did. Your family needs you too, Trisha. You bring them so much joy."

Why do my parents need me? They've got Tommy. That's enough. I want to play in this magical place. The flowers sing. Did you notice that when you visited? I love their songs. And there are red birds and blue ones. Wow, a huge white one just flew past.

"Trisha, your mommy and daddy are very sad. They believe it's their fault that you fell."

How can they think that? They weren't there. I climbed a tree and went too far out on the limb. It's my fault. But it's okay, everything is okay.

"Trisha, honey, I'd love to talk with you in person. I want to tell you about my two kids. Won't you come back for a visit?"

Lady, I like it here. It's so much fun. Everyone is happy.

"Maybe you could come for a short visit?"

A short one? Then I could go back? If it's a short one, I'll do that. But I want to come back to this happy place.

Nurse Laila whispers to Sarah, "We've got a pulse. They're taking her to surgery right now."

Sarah stands back as the medical team pushes the gurney out of the ER and to the elevator. When she sees the distress of the parents, Sarah goes to them to offer comfort.

"Your daughter needs surgery to release the pressure on her brain. Let's move to the waiting area, where it's quieter."

The parents follow Sarah and join her at a small table.

"I saw you talking to Trisha. What did you say?" the mother asks.

"I spoke with her about what I saw when I stopped breathing. And I told her about a choice I made to come back to my family. Keep in mind I couldn't hear anything from your daughter. But I do remember my thoughts when I was unconscious, and I used that memory as a bridge to try to reach her."

"You think she heard you?"

"Absolutely. When I was in her state, I heard everything, but no one heard me."

The father clears his throat. "So, what did you say to help her come back to us?"

"I told her that you needed her, just like my family needed me. I told her that you loved her and blamed yourselves for the accident."

The mother covers her face and sobs. "It was my fault. I should have watched her more closely."

"We always want to blame, especially ourselves, but accidents are accidents. And in your daughter's case, no one is at fault. This is a time for prayers of gratitude." Sarah stands and says, "I'll leave you to yourselves, as I have another appointment. It's been a pleasure meeting you."

The father extends his hand to Sarah and thanks her. "If she lives, it's because of your help."

"Sir, if she lives, it's because she's decided that the joy of being home with you means more to her than heavenly bliss."

After saying her goodbyes, Sarah leaves, deep in thought. *Did I give the right advice? What do I know? Even though I died, medically, how do I know my experience is similar to hers?* She takes the elevator up to Physical Therapy, troubled by her questions. After Sarah finishes her exercises, the physical therapist walks over to her.

"All right, fess up. What's bothering you?"

"It's that obvious?"

"Well, the whole Eeyore thing is a giveaway."

Sarah exhales slowly. "I just spoke with the parents of a child who's now in surgery. I shared my own experience, but . . ."

"But you don't know if it was wise to share as you did? If it was accurate or whether it was similar to this child's experience?"

"Yes, on all counts."

"Were they grateful? Calmer? More hopeful?"

"Yes."

"Then your questions are answered."

"But . . ."

"You can't heal the patients, but love can open the door to its possibility. Do you understand?"

"Thank you. I did what I could. I opened the door."

"Of course, you did. Now go home and enjoy the evening."

···◆◆◆···

Sarah considers the therapist's comments as she walks home. Catching a glimpse of a blooming hydrangea, she marvels at its beauty and wonders if it is her *open door.*

She retrieves her mail and flips through the envelopes, searching for a message from Jack. Upon seeing none, her shoulders fall. She keys open the front door and walks into the empty home. Leaning heavily on the counter, she fights the ever-so-common tears. It's been a long day.

After grabbing a cold bottle of water from the refrigerator, Sarah collapses onto the couch. She sets her water bottle on the floor and stretches across the length of the sofa. Her left hand falls in between a cushion and hits a wadded sheet of paper and a hard object. Sarah pulls out both and gasps as her chest tightens. Shocked by what she holds, Sarah sits up straight and calls her sister-in-law.

"Chrissy, I found something, and it's got me worried."

"I'm here for you. Tell me. Whatever it is, we'll figure things out."

"I noticed a paper tucked between the couch cushions, and when I dislodged it, I discovered it was a crumpled letter from Mateo, and . . ."

"And what?"

"I also found a .357 Magnum bullet."

"You're kidding? Does Jack clean his gun there?"

"Never. He hasn't pulled out his revolver since Bobby's birth. He keeps it locked up. There's more. I went into the bedroom and checked his safe. It was ajar on the shelf."

"So, what do you think?"

"I believe Jack planned to take his life."

"But, but . . ."

"I think his friend's letter changed his mind and that's why he left."

"What was in the letter?"

"Mateo asked Jack to meet him in Burgos. To walk with him on the *Camino de Santiago*."

"Hmm, that makes sense. Jack wasn't himself. Wouldn't talk with anyone. Wouldn't eat. He must have thought Matt could help him. Did you ever meet the guy?"

"No, but Jack mentioned him on occasion. I think he considered him a close friend."

"Yeah, they enlisted together, and then both got assigned to Afghanistan. I haven't seen Matt for years, not since high school. He's a good guy."

Sarah says, "I'm going to meet him, Chrissy."

"You're what?"

"I'm going to Spain to find Jack."

"Seriously?"

"Yes. After we hang up, I'll study the trails and timelines. I need to do this. I need to make sure he's okay."

"Call me as soon as you have any information."

"Will do."

···✦✦✦···

Thirty minutes later, Sarah calls back.

"I've calculated he'll reach the Cathedral within the week. I could fly into Lavacolla, spend the night, and trek the final six miles. I found accommodations close to the Cathedral, so . . ."

"Six miles? Can you do that? And with a backpack on your shoulders?"

"I might be slower than some, but I've built up my strength and completed four miles today. I feel a little sore, but nothing that's concerning. As for the backpack, I read that you can pay to have your luggage delivered to your next stop. It doesn't cost much, so that's what I'll do."

"Hmm. That changes things." Chrissy pauses to think. "You're not going by yourself, sis. I'll come with you."

"I can do it alone."

"Maybe, but not this time. I'm going with you and that's final."

"I recognize that tone, and it's useless to argue with you."

"Yep, totally useless."

"It will be a team effort. I'll reserve a room for the week. But, Chrissy, not a word to anyone—and especially not to my parents. This is need-to-know information."

"I've got to say something because, otherwise, your parents or mine will send out the calvary."

"Can we say we're going on a sister trip? Spa, swimming pool, that kind of thing?"

"That'll work. When do we leave?"

"Tomorrow. We'll take a night flight to Frankfurt, then fly to Lavacolla."

"You don't mess around, do you? I'll pack and tell my folks about our girly adventure and will be at your place by noon."

"I'm excited, aren't you?"

"Excited? I've too much in my head right now to feel excited—starting with I need to make sure my car has a full tank of gas."

"Phoenix isn't that far." Sarah chuckles.

"True, but I don't want to look for a gas station when we fly back. Who knows what time we'll get in? Call your parents, sis. If you don't, they'll call Missing Persons for a full investigation."

"You're too funny, but you're right. I'm on it!"

CHAPTER 21

FINDING JACK

Exhausted by the long flights, Sarah and Chrissy arrive at the Lavacolla Airport jittery and needing something to eat.

Chrissy moans, "I've got to stretch or take a run. My muscles are tied in knots."

'We'll get plenty of exercise tomorrow, sis. Right now, we need to find a cab."

"Okay, I'm looking. What about that white car going through the roundabout? Kinda looks like a cab. Has writing on the side door."

"It's worth a try. Let's wave it over." As the car nears, they signal that they'd like a ride.

They take the cab to a small, nearby pensión. Their driver speaks broken English and, proudly, points out the sights, and shares tidbits about the history of the area. Chrissy attempts to respond in Spanish, but her stumbles result in their collective levity.

After pulling into a cobbled driveway, the man says, "This is your pensión. Good people here. You will be happy."

Sarah and Chrissy thank the driver and pick up their luggage. Waving goodbye, they walk towards the inn. Tucked behind a canopy of oak tree branches, it's barely visible from the road. The matron greets the two travelers and says their beds are prepared for them. She leads them on a meandering stone path, under an arch of vines and creeping flowers, to a courtyard separating the main house from the guest cottage.

The matron explains that only women occupy the cottage, and they can choose from the few remaining beds. She adds, "Breakfast will be served from sunrise onward." With that, she bids them goodbye.

Sarah and Chrissy take a deep breath as they size up what's before them—a room with six single beds. One cot has a backpack thrown on top of it, and two others have jackets draped across the top.

Sarah smiles, "Well, our mini-pilgrimage begins. Let's claim our beds and find something to eat. How about those two cots next to the back wall?" She clambers over backpacks and other personal items of the guests and plops her bag on one of the remaining beds. "This will work, right?"

"Fine by me." Chrissy watches Sarah as she lies down on the bed. "Are you okay?"

"Yeah. A little dizzy, that's all. Long day."

"Did your doctor have anything to say about your lightheadedness?"

"Not really. It's probably residual from the trauma."

"Or you're pregnant."

"Impossible. Why would you say that?"

"You're always lightheaded when you're pregnant." Chrissy laughs.

"This is different, and it's not funny."

"Maybe not, but we can't always be serious. Shall we grab something to eat? That's probably another reason for your dizziness. We haven't eaten for eight hours, maybe more."

"I saw you nibbling."

"Peanuts do not constitute a meal."

"Okay, grumpy, let's go. I need to stretch my legs."

·· ◆ ◆ ◆ ◆ ··

The following morning, rays of rose-colored light glint through the edges of the closed blinds in the cottage. Several pilgrims cluster and talk in hushed voices about their final day on the *Camino*. Sarah sits up and greets them.

"Bueno días, mujer. Americana?"

"Si."

"I can speak English. Have you completed the full *Camino*?"

Sarah shakes her head. "No, we just began. I haven't been well, and I don't have much strength, but I came to meet my husband. He started in Burgos. This is his sister." She points to Chrissy, who stirs in her bed.

"Welcome to you both. The *Camino* is for everyone. May it bless you."

"Thank you for your kindness."

"My friends and I leave now. Maybe we'll meet you later."

The four women strap on their backpacks and wave goodbye. Sarah reaches over to Chrissy and taps her on the shoulder.

"Hey, are you awake yet?"

"Do I have a choice?"

"Are you kidding me? Everyone's gone but us. Breakfast is waiting. The sun is shining. What more do you want?"

"Eh, nothing, really. I'm getting up." On her feet, she stretches in all directions, yawns, and says, "I wonder what's for breakfast. I can smell the aroma of coffee."

"I was thinking the same. I need a cup or two. Let's get dressed and find the kitchen."

⋯⋅◆⋅⋯

After their morning meal, Sarah speaks to the proprietor about her luggage and arranges for it to be delivered to the hotel in Santiago de Compostela. Chrissy sits and revels in another cup of coffee while watching pilgrims hike past the window.

Sarah settles back in her chair and takes another sip of coffee. "It's all set. My luggage will be delivered to the hotel. Other than my shoulder bag, I don't have to carry anything. Are you sure you don't want your backpack delivered as well?"

"Positive. I feel like a pilgrim with it strapped to my back." Chrissy sits up straight and acts like she's praying.

"You're too much. And I'm pretty sure you're being sacrilegious, but you're also hilarious."

"Maybe it's God-like to laugh. Ever think of that?"

"Nope, but I think it's time for us to go."

"All right. Let me get my backpack, and I'm ready."

Sarah and Chrissy set off on their six-mile walk among several other hikers on the tree-lined *Camino* path. A creek babbles nearby and offers the illusion of coolness. But the hot sun reminds them that it's summer. Sweat rolls down the side of Sarah's face. And after the first mile, she pauses under a eucalyptus tree.

"You doing okay, sis? Too hot?"

"I'll be fine in a minute, a little lightheaded is all."

"Are you sure you're not . . ."

"Hey. Stop that. It's not funny. I'm *definitely* not pregnant, and I don't want you to mention it again."

"Calm down. I was going to suggest that you're probably dehydrated. You need to take off your sweatshirt and drink some water. It's way too hot in the sun."

Sarah studies her friend. "Were you really going to say that?"

Chrissy responds with a mischievous smile. "Are you suggesting I'm a liar?"

"Forget about it. I'll drink, and we can go."

"Stop trying to be a hero. There's no need to push yourself. Let's sit for a while and people-watch. See that fallen tree trunk on the embankment? We can rest there. It's in full view of the pilgrims' path."

"I'm not trying to be a hero."

"If you say so." Chrissy gives her a playful shove. "I want to watch the show. Hordes of pilgrims have passed by. Some speak French, others German or Italian, or Spanish. I've even heard a few Slavic languages and, of course, some English. It's the United Nations parading past us."

Sarah laughs and gives her friend a thumbs up. "I'm ready. Let's go claim that tree trunk."

When they crest the hill named the *Monte do Gozo*, they spot the three spires of the Cathedral of Santiago.

"What an incredible view," Chrissy exclaims. "Someday, I might come back and actually hike the whole *Camino*."

The two find a comfortable spot next to tall ferns and a forest of evergreen trees. A cool breeze weaves through the tree branches and lifts Sarah's hat off her head. Chrissy picks it up for her.

Sarah says, "Thanks. Since we're settled, I've got a little something for you."

"Am I supposed to guess?"

"Nope. It's in my shoulder bag." Sarah reaches inside and pulls out the secret item wrapped in a napkin. "Here you go."

Chrissy looks at her friend suspiciously and opens the napkin. "You stole the churros?"

"Didn't steal. They were on the table this morning, and since we didn't eat them, I pocketed them."

"Fair enough. I'm suddenly voraciously hungry. How about you?"

Sarah laughs at her friend. "Oh course, I'm always hungry for a pastry."

Chrissy stretches and waves to a few pilgrims. "This is nice. Sitting under this oak tree, eating these long rolls of fried dough, watching all the people trudge down to the cathedral square. Did you notice the old lady with a cane? I think that must have been her daughter with her. So sweet."

"Remember what the traveler at the pensión said to us? 'The *Camino* is for everyone.' I think that means folks of all ages and abilities."

"How are you doing? Feeling better?"

"I'm ready. Let's get on the path again."

They start down the hill and are surprised when they hear someone call out in English, "Hey, blondie, don't I know you?"

Chrissy swivels and squints at the bronzed man with close-cropped dark black hair. "Mateo?"

"Yeah, so what are you doing here?" He pulls off his sunglasses and sticks them in his shirt pouch. "The last time I was with your family, you were a junior in high school, begging your mom to let you go to the prom."

Chrissy blushes at the comment. "Of course, that's how you'd remember me. I recall that day well, sans the begging. You and Jack were leaving for Basic Training."

"True. So back to my original question, what are you doing in Compostela?" He eases a little closer and jams his hands into his front pockets.

"I could ask you the same, Mr. Inquisitor, but if you must know, I came with Sarah to help her find Jack."

"Huh, and I thought you came to be with me." He smirks playfully and continues to tease. "Jack's behind me a few minutes, moaning about blisters. I told him I was going ahead of him because I was tired of listening to him."

"You didn't."

"Yeah, I did. The final steps are always the hardest. And we've all got to walk them alone. And look, he's doing just fine by himself." He rolls his eyes mischievously and points to the ridge behind them.

Sarah looks up the hill and observes Jack as he hobbles down the trail. His usual stubble is now a full beard, crowding his otherwise sunburnt skin. She calls out, waving wildly. "Jack! Over here!"

Immediately, Jack peers in the direction of Sarah's voice and, finding her, he drops his backpack and runs to swoop her into his arms.

Mateo reaches for Chrissy. "Well heck, you need a hug too. I don't want you standing there all alone."

Matt wraps his arms around Chrissy, and she bursts into giggles. His playful stunts and laid-back manner always did put her at ease.

When they hear Jack's sobs, they both turn.

"I'm so, so sorry," Jack says. "I wish I could have done more. When your doctor explained the probabilities related to a lengthy coma, I was beside myself. I couldn't deal with another funeral, and coming home to an empty house every night was worse than hell. No children begging for cookies or juice or a bottle. I tried, but I couldn't do it."

"Jack, there's nothing to forgive. I'm so grateful to be with you, the love of my life."

Matt interrupts and reminds them about the Pilgrim's Mass. "It's time, but if you two need to talk more, Chrissy and I can attend. Whatever's best for you."

Sarah says, "Jack and I should be there. Let's all go. We can talk later. Can't we, dear?"

"I'm with you either way."

Matt bends and whispers to Chrissy, "I knew that would get them going."

"Are you always this bad?"

"Eh . . . maybe." He smiles impishly and grabs her hand.

As they hike down into the plaza, they join groups of pilgrims arriving from all directions. Street musicians add festivity to the masses of young and old who now finish their pilgrimage.

··•◆•···

Seated in a crowded pew midway up the nave of the Cathedral of Santiago de Compostela, the four listen intently as the priest reads from chapter six of the Gospel of Matthew. Mateo translates for his friends. At the end of the reading, the cleric begins his sermon by rereading one line, *"Look at the birds of the air; they do not sow or reap or store away in barns, and yet your heavenly Father feeds them. Are you not much more valuable than they?"* (Matthew 6:26, NIV)

The priest pauses and contemplates the gathering of pilgrims. "You've traveled many miles to reach this holy destination. Some of you came side-by-side with friends, but most of you backpacked with strangers. All of you were accompanied by *the birds of the air*. Beautiful and free, these little creatures aren't bound by expectations or fear. They soar through the heavens in ecstasy.

"Before you leave to go back to your country, your home, or your job, take time to listen to your heart. Did you find what you came here to find? Or did something deeper stir in your soul? What did our loving God say to you along the *Camino?* These are important questions. Ones worthy of great reflection. Maybe you found reasons to hope. Maybe you made new friends. Maybe you realized you need very little to be happy.

"Take time, dear followers of the Way of St. James, to answer this one important question. Did you find what you were looking for?"

Matt sits silent, deep in thought. Jack shoves him. "What did he say?"

"He asked, did you find what you were looking for?"

Jack looks at Sarah and meets her eyes with tenderness. He squeezes her hand and whispers, "I found what I was searching for. You're all I've ever wanted."

As he stares up into the vastness of the Cathedral, Jack focuses on the *botafumeiro*, a giant ancient censer, which hangs from the dome of the church. In the early centuries, it fumigated the environment, but today—symbolically—it clears his soul. With his eyes closed, Jack travels back to Afghanistan and to the little children, he couldn't save. He tells them he loves them and, with his mind's eye, watches as they fade away. Next, he travels to the accident scene. Jack wipes tears from his closed eyelids, kisses each of his children, and watches them float happily into the heavens. When he opens his eyes, he gazes afresh at Sarah, and whispers, "They are in heaven, aren't they?"

"Yes, and they're happy."

He glances at Chrissy, who sits next to him in the pew, and discovers that his closest friend holds his sister's hand. At that moment, blissful contentment washes over Jack, and he sits at peace.

·· ◆ ◆ ◆ ◆ ··

After the service, Mateo exits the cathedral hand in hand with Chrissy. He tells her, "I'm continuing the trek to Cape Finisterre."

Chrissy slows and asks, "Is this something you need to do alone?"

"No. You interested in a real hike?" A coltish grin teases.

"Might be. Is that a problem?"

"Hmm, do you whine like your brother?"

"OMG, you're a pain. No, I have my own ways of whining, and I'm accustomed to getting what I want!"

"Interesting. Does that include babysitting you?"

"We're long past those days, Mr. Silva. I don't need babysitting."

"All right then. Let's find out if we can hike the sixty-five miles to the Atlantic without any major incidents. Where's your gear?"

"This is all I have. I only packed for a couple of days."

Matt crinkles his nose. "That could be a problem."

Chrissy gives him a spirited shove as Jack and Sarah approach.

"What's going on here?" Jack asks.

"Not much." Matt smiles. "Only planning our hike to the ocean."

"No way!" Jack gawks at each of them.

"Yep, don't know how far we'll get, but if Miss Prissy can hold her own, I'm in."

"You'll give up before I do," Chrissy snaps.

"I'll take that as a bet, and you're on."

Sarah raises her eyebrows. "This will be interesting, but knowing you both, I think it will be a tie. How far is it?"

"A four or five-day journey. Of course, with Miss—"

"Don't you dare call me *prissy*."

"Wasn't going to say that. I was considering Miss Perfect."

They all laugh and say their goodbyes. But before going their separate ways, Chrissy hands Jack her car keys and explains where she parked at the airport. "Tell Mom and Dad I'm fine. Say I needed a longer adventure. And if you don't need your sleeping bag, I just might."

CHAPTER 22

A SURPRISE DIAGNOSIS

Wrapped in each other's arms, Jack and Sarah fly to Frankfurt, where they wait for their connecting flight to Phoenix.

Sarah speaks softly into Jack's ear, "There's something I need to tell you."

"Anything. I'm here for you."

"My heart stopped beating during surgery, and the doctor called the time of death."

"I didn't know that. No one told me."

"What's important is what happened during that brief time. I saw the babies."

"What do you mean you saw them?"

Sarah considers her surroundings and, respectful of the nearby passengers, whispers, "I was with them briefly. They ran around in a field of flowers. They were so happy, Jack. I still hear their laughter. They called out to me and waved. We were together briefly."

"How do you know that was real?"

"I can't give you proof, but I can describe the surgery, the interactions between the doctors and nurses. I can tell you about my death. And I saw you in the waiting room and felt your despair. You're the reason I came back. I couldn't let you manage the tragedy alone."

Jack pulls her closer. "I came close to joining our babies."

"I suspected as much."

"You did?"

"Yeah. I found a bullet between the couch cushions. I knew you hadn't opened the gun safe since before Bobby was born, so I suspected the worst." Her eyes soften. "And I understood."

"I, ah, I . . ."

"You don't need to explain. Obviously, it scared the heck out of me, but thankfully, I also found a wadded letter from Mateo. And Chrissy shared your postcard. I put the two together and concluded you'd gone with him on the *Camino*. I had to find you to relieve the suffering I felt you carried deep inside."

"I don't know what to say. I wasn't in the right state of mind. I was all mixed up and couldn't find a reason to live."

"Do you, now?"

"How can you ask me that? Of course, I do. I have you."

"But what if I wasn't here? Would you still have a reason to live?"

Jack digs in his back pocket and pulls out a document. "This gives me a reason. As I walked the *Camino*, officials stamped my Certificado. It proves I completed the journey, but to me, it's a reminder that I climbed out of death's grip and discovered the gift of life. If I ever have doubts again, I'll return to the *Camino de Santiago*."

"And I'll hike it with you."

··◆◆◆◆◆··

On the fifteen-hour flight to Arizona, Jack and Sarah fall asleep. All is calm until the last hour of the trip. A sudden drop in altitude frightens the passengers. Even worse, the hot high winds rock the plane and cause the overhead bins to rattle loudly while the engines churn. Sarah grabs Jack's hand and holds it tightly. The plane descends further into the Phoenix Sky Harbor International Airport, and hits the runway hard, throwing everyone forward in their seats.

"Not quite the landing I hoped for, but we're twenty-five minutes early. That's a plus. Right, Jack? We'll be home sooner than expected."

"It won't be the same, but together we can bring it to life again. And, maybe . . ."

"Another baby?" Sarah asks. "I've wondered about that."

Jack leans his head next to Sarah's and kisses her. "Today we begin our new lives. Do you remember where Chrissy parked her car? Her directions were a bit skimpy."

"I think I can find it pretty easily. It's in the garage next to our terminal."

"Okay, I'll follow your lead. Let's pick up our stuff and head home."

··•◆•··

Two hours later, Jack and Sarah pull into their driveway and stare at their house. Other than the light from the streetlamp beaming through their cypress tree, the home is dark on this moonless night.

Jack hesitates, but Sarah takes his hand. "Let's go in together. I think our home needs us."

Jack nods his agreement, then says, "Someone mowed the grass for us. I need to thank our neighbors. They've all been so kind."

"My dad told me he'd take care of the yard."

"You're, you're serious? Really?"

"Yes, really. He was absolutely sincere when he promised."

"What brought this on?"

"A hospital conversation between Mom and me." Sarah raises her eyebrows and smiles.

"It must have been a doozy."

"We'll talk about it later." Sarah inserts the door key. "Are you ready?"

Jack shrugs, and they step into the house. Sarah flips on the lights, and they scan the space in disbelief. The entire living area is spotless. Sarah notices a message on the kitchen counter. It's from her parents. *Welcome home, dear. Don't worry about a thing. We're a family, and we're here for you. Much love, Mom and Dad.*

Sarah opens the refrigerator and looks wide-eyed at shelves stocked with everything they might need. She turns to Jack, falls into his arms, and sobs tears that she's long repressed. "Chrissy must have called my mom and let her know we were coming home. She probably told her where we keep the extra key."

Sarah glances at the monthly calendar on the side of the fridge and asks Jack, "What day is it?"

He checks his watch. "June twenty-first."

"I have an appointment with my surgeon tomorrow morning. I totally forgot about it."

"I'll come with you. Whatever lies ahead of us, we'll face it together."

···◆◆◆···

The following morning at 8 a.m., Jack and Sarah stroll hand-in-hand to the hospital to meet with Dr. Roberts. They take the elevator to the fourth floor and go directly to his office. With a quick knock, they are welcomed in and ushered to a conference table.

"Good to see you both," the surgeon says. "Come on in and have a seat."

Jack glances out the window at the park. "You've got a great view."

"One of the best. If only I could enjoy it more." He scoots into his chair, leans back, and pulls out the X-rays and reports. "Shall we get started?"

"Yes, please," Sarah says.

"I hope you're doing well, Sarah. You certainly appear refreshed."

"I feel great, Doctor. The dizzy spells are rarer, and I don't have any complaints, other than putting on a little extra weight."

"Still moving around well?"

"We walked here, and I had no problems at all."

"Good to hear. Let's go over the results of the blood work. Just so you won't worry, everything is positive. You're in normal ranges for all the indicators. Only one stood out."

Jack reaches for Sarah's hand and focuses intently on the physician.

"When I ordered the blood tests, I didn't want to leave any stone uncovered, so I ordered a beta-hCG assay."

Sarah arches her eyebrows. "A pregnancy test?"

"I wanted to make sure, and it's a good thing I did. The nausea and dizziness you've mentioned to me are probably because you're about four months pregnant."

"What? Are you sure? I, ah, I don't know how that could be. That would mean . . ."

"You were pregnant before the accident. And it seems the baby survived the impact and subsequent surgery. I've set up an ultrasound today, to make sure the fetus is developing normally. You've gone through a lot, and the baby endured every up and down of your experience. I've asked Dr. Taylor to assist with your case, and she will join us in radiology in ten minutes. Because she's a neonatal surgeon, she'll know how to proceed if there's any concern."

Sarah takes a deep breath. "This is unexpected, but of course, let's do this."

Jack says, "Yesterday we talked of more children, but this—this is most unexpected."

Within minutes, the threesome takes the elevator to the Radiology Department. Sarah is ushered into the imaging room and gets comfortable on the table. When Dr. Taylor arrives, she talks briefly to Dr. Roberts and introduces herself to Sarah.

"I'm sorry about your loss, Sarah. I understand only too well how devastating it is to lose a child. My first baby died of SIDS. Not only did I grieve her passing, but I also lived with profound guilt because I'm a doctor and could do nothing to save her. Only with the birth of my second and third child did that pain ease. So, today, I hope your sorrows will lift with the good news of a baby on the way."

"Thank you so much, Doctor. I'm lost for words." Sarah wipes away her tears, as Jack kisses his wife on her forehead.

"Let's begin." Carefully, Dr. Taylor maneuvers the instrument over Sarah's uterus. She stops, adds more conductor gel, and begins again. She stops once more and eases the instrument lower, then to the side, and back again.

Sarah tightens her clasp on Jack's hand as she watches the neonatal surgeon's reactions. "Is something wrong, Doctor?"

"Nothing's wrong, but I need to recheck a few measurements." The doctor starts to explain and then grows silent as she steadies the fetal doppler and turns up the volume. "Hear that faint thumping sound? That's your baby's heartbeat." She shifts the instrument and adds, "Hear this one? It's your second baby's heartbeat. You're having twins."

CHAPTER 23

UNEXPECTED SETTLEMENT

Jack and Sarah leave the hospital, bewildered by the news that they'll soon be parents again.

Sarah flushes pink at the thought and says, "I feel like a giddy kid. I'm speechless. I'd jump up and down, but I don't think that's wise right now."

Jack stops mid-stride. "And I feel like I'm in a dream and need to wake up, but I don't want to." With arms outstretched, he embraces his wife and whispers, "I love you so much. Everything is going to work out. I know that now."

The two chat excitedly and when they reach their street, they call out hellos to a few neighbors.

"It's so good you're both back home again! We've missed you."

"All is well, and we're here for good. We look forward to getting together with you soon."

Jack opens the door and follows Sarah into their home. He no sooner closes the door than his phone rings.

"Dad?"

"Hey, son, glad you're home."

"I planned to call you today. Chrissy asked me to tell you that she'll be back home in a few days. She extended her trip."

"She's needed a break, so this is good."

"Dad, I'm sorry I kept you in the dark. I'll explain more in person. It was a spur-of-the-moment decision, and I simply packed my bag and left. My head wasn't on straight, but it is now."

"You don't need to explain, Jack. Sometimes getting away is the best way to clear our thoughts. But when you're ready, there's something important I need to discuss with you. The sooner the better."

"That sounds mysterious. Any time is fine with me. Would you like to come here?"

"In two hours?"

"Works for me. See you in two."

Jack glances over at Sarah. "This isn't like him. Something must have happened."

"Maybe he wants to help. He could have a spare car for us to use."

"That's a possibility, but I don't think so."

"I'll make some muffins real fast and prepare a pot of coffee. At least you can talk and sip at the same time. Oh, and about our news. Shall we wait until we're more settled?"

"Uh-huh, let's wait. We could invite our families to come for a barbecue in another month."

"I love that idea. Another month it is."

····◆◆◆◆◆····

Good to his word, Mr. Jameson pulls into his son's driveway exactly two hours later. With a limp, the balding man shuffles to the front door, carrying a large manila envelope. Jack steps out on the porch and greets him with a buddy hug.

"It's so good to see you, Dad. Come on in."

"It warms my heart to know you're okay. I was worried, son, but you appear rested and happy. Couldn't have imagined anything better than this."

"Thank you, Dad. It's been rough, but things are on the upswing now. Shall we sit at the table?"

The two men settle into the squeaky chairs, and Sarah brings over cinnamon muffins and offers coffee.

"Thank you, dear. I could use a cup of coffee, and I never pass up a muffin. Maybe you could join us? What I need to say applies to you as well."

Sarah flinches and glances at Jack and her father-in-law. "Are you sure? I don't want to interfere with your time together."

"Not at all, so please, sit with us. Once you're comfortable, I'll explain." Mr. Jameson clears his throat, strokes his bushy eyebrows, and wipes the sweat from his deeply lined forehead. He pulls papers from the envelope and looks at Jack steadily.

"Soon after the accident, your mom asked me to find a personal injury lawyer for you. That was easy to do. I got hold of my friend Charlie Rutherford because he managed the legal matters for the Force when I was working. Anyway, he reviewed your case and said he'd handle it himself. His exact words were, 'It's an open and shut case,' and he was right.

"Charlie met with the attorneys representing LTP Truckers and the furniture company. They expected to be contacted, and they were aware of their liability. The process went silent until yesterday. Charlie came over to the house with this document. It's an out-of-court settlement. That's why I'm here."

Jack furrows his brow. "I vaguely remember the coroner mentioning the need for an attorney, but I'd forgotten all about it. Thank you, Dad, for taking this on and helping us."

"It's nothing. Charlie did everything, but I was grateful to help in my own small way. The financial offer will surprise you."

Jack's father sets the settlement agreement in front of the young couple and laces his fingers. "There's a lot of legal gibberish in this, but it's the second paragraph that's important. If you accept the mentioned compensation in that paragraph and sign the document, there will be no court hearing. The legal proceeding will be over."

He points to the second paragraph. "Read this section carefully."

Jack and Sarah read the indicated text, then read it again, and stare blankly at Jack's father.

"Five million dollars, Dad?"

"Yes, son. Five million dollars. You both need to decide if you want to settle this quickly or proceed with legal action."

Jack and Sarah glance at each other and nod. "We'll sign today. We need to put this behind us and move forward."

"I'm glad to hear it, son. It's possible you could get a bigger settlement, but it would be an agonizing process."

Sarah says, "I'm overwhelmed and don't know what to say." Her voice trembles, "This is an immense relief. Thank you for stepping in on our behalf."

"I was happy to do so, and as I said earlier, my part was easy."

Jack bites his lower lip and wipes his eyes. "You've always been a great dad to me. I don't have the words to thank you properly, except to live a life you'd be proud of."

Mr. Jameson reaches and puts his hand on Jack's shoulder. "I've been proud of you since the day you were born. You're everything I've ever wanted in a son. I can't protect you from life's challenges, but you've shown me I don't need to. You've handled every hurdle put before you with dignity. Afghanistan took its toll, but even there you met those challenges bravely."

Jack rubs his hand against the jagged scar running down his cheek. "Sometimes it wasn't easy, but I gave it my all. Then, after the accident, I was back in the war zone again. I didn't know what was real and what wasn't. That's why I left, Dad. I had to get straight."

"I figured as much. You were with Mateo, right?"

"Yeah. Couldn't ask for a better friend. He'd written and invited me to join him on the *Camino de Santiago*. Said we could meet in Burgos, Spain. I was a mess, and his letter was the only hope I had. So, within a few minutes, I packed my bag and headed out. I didn't tell anyone because I couldn't deal with questions or concerns. I could barely deal with myself. Anyway, I found him, and over the next weeks, he helped me get my head together. He forced me to face my life and see clearly." Jack smiles and adds, "The guy can be merciless."

Jack's father taps his fingers on the table. "Chrissy's with him, yes?"

"Correct. They hit it off right away. When we said goodbye, they told us they planned to hike to the ocean and then head back to the States. My guess is they'll return in another eight to ten days."

"I always liked him and was glad you were in Basic Training together. I knew he'd have your back and vice versa."

"Hmm . . . you might end up seeing more of him."

His dad gives Jack the eye and belly laughs. "If that happens, I'll be happy. I can imagine those two together—fireworks and all."

CHAPTER 24

THE OFFER

Sarah eases out of bed, but not before Jack gives her belly a smooch. At almost five months pregnant, she can no longer hide the twins with a loose shirt.

"It's time to unpack my maternity clothes. These babies need space." She takes Jack's hand and places it on the side of her bulging abdomen. "Can you feel that? Tiny kicks?"

"Umm, maybe. I'm not sure. I'm happy you can, though. Have you thought about names?"

"A little. If the obstetrician is right and we're having boys, we could name them after our dads, or not. Do you have names in mind?"

"Yes and no. I've thought about James."

"After your Marine friend, Jimmy?"

"Yeah. I haven't gotten any further than that."

"Well, my Dad's middle name is James. What's your Dad's middle name?"

"Thomas."

"James and Thomas. I like that. Two strong biblical names, and grand-fathers who would love a namesake."

Jack wraps his arms around Sarah. "Shall we announce it at the barbe-cue tomorrow?"

"Absolutely. The pregnancy and the names—it will be quite the surprise!"

"By the way, Mateo texted me this morning. He and Chrissy got back the night before last and will be coming to the barbecue. I think wedding bells might be in the works."

"Wouldn't that be wonderful?"

"Yeah. He'd be family for real then."

"Don't forget, I'm meeting with Dr. Roberts this morning about a hospital matter. Want to give me a lift?"

"Sure. I need to pick up a few things at the grocery store and can drop you off on the way. Thirty minutes, sound good?"

"Perfect."

··•✦•✦•··

Sarah takes the elevator to the fourth floor, where many of the physicians have offices. Dr. Roberts stands in the hallway, talking with a man on crutches. When he notices Sarah, he motions for her to come join him.

"Sarah, this is perfect timing. Benjamin stopped by to meet with me and mentioned how you helped him when he was incapacitated. You should hear his comments directly. If you have the time, let's go into the conference room." Dr. Roberts leads the way and offers them a seat.

Positioned directly across from each other, Benjamin focuses on Sarah and says, "I'm grateful to meet you finally."

"And I'm happy to know you're doing well. You were in a coma the last time we met."

"Yes, but I heard every word you said. You told me that I wasn't alone and to listen to your voice. So, I did."

"I hope it helped in some small way."

"You're the reason I'm here. One of your comments melted my heart. You said, 'Every love you've ever known awaits you. Every tender exchange is yours to experience again.' At that moment, I realized I hadn't taken time for love. My life was my work, and my work didn't involve love.

"Ms. Sarah, because of what you said that day, I fought to live, to regain consciousness. I want to experience love—in this life."

"Mr. O'Malley."

"Please, call me Ben."

"Ben, I'm sure love awaits you. It's not something we need to chase. It finds us when we're ready to receive."

"Do you have any advice for me? About how I can help make that happen?"

"I'm probably not the best person to offer advice, but I'd suggest doing things that feed your soul. For example, you can go to the lake and sit at the water's edge. Just be still and listen to the geese, to the sound of kayak oars hitting the water, to the rustle of leaves from the alder and willow trees. If you do that, your worries will fade, and time will shift to the present."

Ben stares at Sarah and, eventually, manages a response. "I'm not sure I understand, but I want to."

"Love is everywhere present, Ben, but our busy minds keep us from recognizing that truth. You might consider joining a local meditation group. Getting accustomed to silence takes a bit, but once you do, a beautiful world opens. And who knows, you might meet a special someone."

Ben laughs at her comment. "That's an incentive for sure." A few minutes later, he stands and says his goodbyes. "You both have much important work to do, so I'll let you be. I hope we meet again, perhaps along the lake. And Sarah, I'm forever grateful for your guidance."

Dr. Roberts watches the man disappear down the hall, then turns and grins at Sarah. "You have an amazing gift. I wasn't expecting Ben, but I'm sure glad he visited. He affirms what I want to address. See this card?" He holds it up and gives it to Sarah. "It's from the parents of the child who fell from a tree and suffered brain trauma."

"I remember her—Trisha."

"Her parents wrote to me to ask that I thank the kind woman who helped their daughter. They say their child talks about the lady who encouraged her to return to her parents. Sound familiar? They also included a donation for the hospital endowment."

Sarah chokes up and takes a deep breath. "Yes, it's familiar. Sometimes, we wonder if we're making a difference, and then a simple card arrives."

"Which brings me to the reason I asked you to meet with me. I want to formalize your patient outreach. I don't have a title for the position yet, but if you're willing to carry on as you have, accompanying our patients in their last hours, I'll meet with the CEO. In this role, you'd continue to offer direct care to our patients, but you'd also train our medical teams on how to speak with a comatose patient. Who better to do that than you?"

Sarah's eyes glisten in an unfocused gaze. Her cheeks flush, and a relaxed smile spreads across her lips. "Dr. Roberts, I'd love to serve in this new role."

CHAPTER 25

THE BARBECUE

Red-faced, Jack stands over the barbecue grill. The charcoal burns hot, almost ready for the ribs and chicken. With the sun directly overhead, there's no escaping the heat. Jack's T-shirt sticks to his back and beads of sweat run down his forehead. He reaches into the cooler for a can of soda and brushes away an irritating bee.

The neighbor's Australian Shepherd yelps a *hello* and runs back and forth along her side of the old picket fence.

"Can't play with you now, Bertha. Later, maybe."

The neighbor calls out, "Sorry about that, Jack. Is she bothering you? I can bring her inside."

"Naw, Fred, she's being friendly is all. We've got family coming over in an hour, and I'm getting the grill ready."

"Give me a shout if she becomes a pain, and I'll bring her in. The pups are due in a few weeks, so she's antsy."

"Will do, but don't worry about it."

Jack takes a break from the grill and struts over to the curious dog. He strokes her black and white fur and says, "You're going to be a mommy soon, huh? I'm going to be a daddy." He flashes back to Charlie, his Labrador Retriever when he was a kid, and remembers the games they played. Caught up in this memory, he wonders if his boys would like a puppy.

Sarah wanders outside and notices his smile. "Did you find some gold coins?"

"No, but maybe. What do you think about getting a puppy for our boys?"

"I thought you were against having a pet."

"Well, I gave in for the goldfish."

Sarah chuckles. "That doesn't count. But since you've mentioned it, I think a puppy, maybe two, would be great."

"We have a few months to think about it, but if the opportunity arises . . ."

"Okay, fess up. You already have pups in mind, don't you?"

"Maybe." An impish grin crosses Jack's face. "Bertha's pregnant."

"Oh, my goodness. I didn't know that. Did you talk to Fred about the puppies?"

"No. He just told me she's pregnant. I had no idea. But the arrangement is ideal, don't you think? We're neighbors. Their mom is on the other side of the fence. Pretty copasetic."

"And you'll promise to house-train the pup or pups?"

"I didn't say that, but *yes*, I will."

"It's a deal! By the way, I came out to tell you that your mom called and said your dad's friend, Charlie Rutherford, is coming with them today."

"The attorney who helped us, right?"

"That's the one."

"Great. It will be good to meet him in person. How are things going in the kitchen?"

"I'm getting there. Baked beans in the oven, corn on the cob ready for the grill, and the potato salad is almost finished. My mom is bringing her prized coleslaw dish. You'll love it. And I have an assortment of different breads. Sound good?"

"Sounds delicious. And dessert?"

"I almost forgot. Your family is bringing two cobblers. Peach and berry. And I've ice cream in the freezer."

"It's hard to believe, isn't it? Our two families sharing a meal together after all the years of tiptoeing around. Which reminds me, I'm not sure we have enough lawn furniture." He counts the chairs and calls over to Sarah. "We're short two."

"What about the folding chairs in the basement?"

"I forgot we had those. I'll fetch them now."

While Jack runs into the house and down to the basement, Sarah strolls over to the fence and talks to Bertha. "Mom to mom, how are you doing my friend? Would you mind if we adopted two of your babies?"

She reaches between two loose posts and strokes Bertha's mane and rubs her belly.

Jack clamors out of the house with the metal chairs. "Got them," he shouts as he climbs down the back steps. "We're set."

Sarah turns and smiles lovingly at her husband. Her eyes sparkle at seeing him so happy. "By the way, Bertha and I have a pact. We're going to protect each other's babies."

"Does this mean what I think it means?"

"Yep, if Fred is fine with it, we'll adopt."

··+♦+··

Two hours later, the charred scent of barbecue sauce spreads across the neighborhood as does backyard laughter. Under the cloudless sky, two families, long estranged, gather and leave their differences behind.

Sarah stands to the side and watches in amazement. Jack's dad and her father share stories next to the swing set. Each with a can of beer in his hand, they laugh heartily. Her mom and Jack's mom arrange the desserts on the side table and chatter, excitedly, like best friends. Chrissy and Mateo cuddle next to the fence and talk to Bertha. Jack nurses the ribs on the grill and discusses the settlement with the attorney.

Then she hears them—her babies. Bobby and Marci. They laugh and run between the family members. *They're here,* she thinks. *They're the ones who brought us together.*

Smoke shimmers from the barbecue and rises toward the heavens. Sarah follows the wisps of gray as they disappear into the atmosphere. Her eyes rest on a pair of doves that fly overhead, and her features soften as she realizes little Bobby and Marci work miracles from heaven. She longs to hold them, but her yearning is not theirs. The babies live happily. Death freed them to play forever in the Light.

ABOUT GWEN M. PLANO

Gwen M. Plano, aka Gwendolyn M. Plano, spent most of her professional life in higher education. Recently retired, she now lives in the high desert of Arizona, where she writes, gardens, and travels with her husband.

Gwen's first book is an acclaimed memoir, *Letting Go into Perfect Love*. Her second book, *The Contract between heaven and earth*, is a thriller fiction novel, co-authored by John W. Howell. It has received multiple awards and is an Amazon Best Seller. *The Choice, the unexpected heroes* is the sequel to *The Contract*. The third book in the series, *The Culmination, a new beginning* is an action-packed military thriller that involves the threat of World War III. The series underscores the belief that only love can change the fate of humanity. In keeping with that theme, *Redemption, A Father's Fatal Decision* focuses on the choice a father makes to protect his family. Gwen's newly released novella, *The Gift*, is a story of three families who meet unexpectedly and rediscover the importance of love.

When Gwen is not writing, she's often in the beautiful Red Rocks of Sedona, where she finds inspiration and peace.

Fresh Ink Group

Independent Multi-media Publisher

Fresh Ink Group / Push Pull Press
Voice of Indie / GeezWriter

Hardcovers
Softcovers
All Ebook Formats
Audiobooks
Podcasts
Worldwide Distribution

Indie Author Services
Book Development, Editing, Proofing
Graphic/Cover Design
Video/Trailer Production
Website Creation
Social Media Marketing
Writing Contests
Writers' Blogs

Authors
Editors
Artists
Experts
Professionals

FreshInkGroup.com
info@FreshInkGroup.com
Twitter: @FreshInkGroup
Facebook.com/FreshInkGroup
LinkedIn: Fresh Ink Group

The Harbor Pointe Inn has loomed on California's cliffs for generations of Hawthornes. For some, it's been a blessing. For others, a curse. Travel through two centuries of stories to discover the old inn's secrets.

In an innocent 1958 American suburb, Shelly doesn't know the power of a kiss. Or how it will change her entire life. At sixteen years old, she falls in love with a young man. One night—just one night—they go too far. Months later, pregnant and shamed, Shelly's parents banish her. Alone and heavily pregnant, circumstances force Shelly to cross the country in an old pickup. A mistaken turn leaves her lost in a forest amidst a severe snow storm and in labor. In the dark of night. Shelly must get help for her new-born baby before they both perish. A light in the distance gives her the slimmest glimmer of hope. After Shelly wraps the infant in her father's old jacket, she trudges through the snow to a lighthouse keeper's cottage. Snow half buries the squat stone building. Will Shelly find shelter, or is it the beginning of the end?

Amazon Kindle Ebook!

Family secrets can be deadly. When Lisa visits her parents one fateful Saturday morning, she hugs her father and takes her suitcase to her childhood bedroom. The doorbell rings, and one minute later, her father lies dead on the floor— three bullets to the chest. The death of Eric Holmes sends shockwaves throughout the quiet neighbor- hood. But for the Holmes family, it is devastating. In this fast-paced psychological thriller, Lisa and her brother embark on a quest to solve the mystery of their father's murder. The journey takes them into a secret world where nothing is as it seems. Once the puzzle pieces begin to coalesce, they realize that their father had multiple lives.

As the facts unravel, the siblings discover the true meaning of *Redemption.*

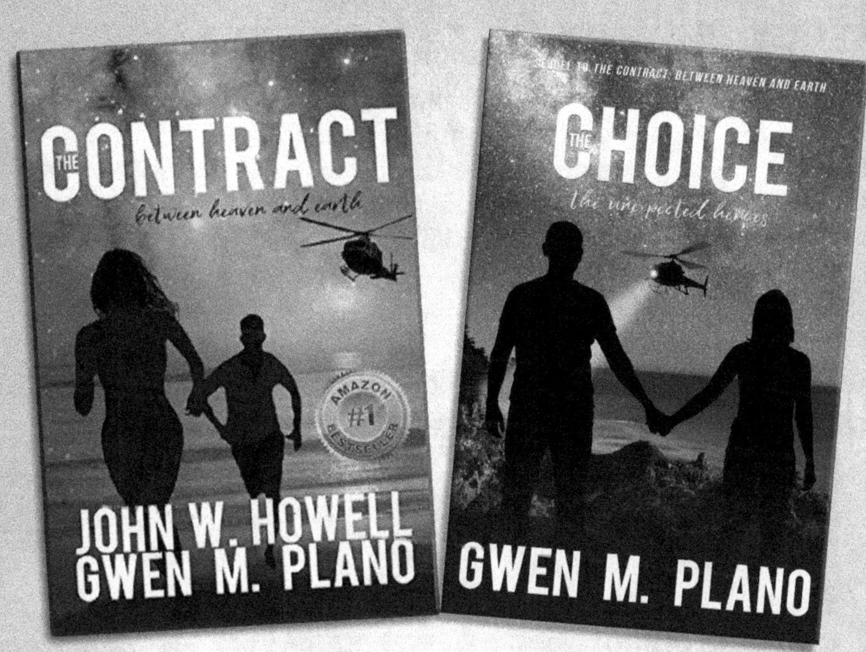

Paranormal, Romantic, Spiritual Thriller Trilogy!

Printed in the USA
CPSIA information can be obtained
at www.ICGtesting.com
LVHW011248270224
772865LV00001B/80